WARM, FOR CHRISTMAS

To Vicki —

Please enjoy
this story — and
pass it on.

George Hyak

WARM, FOR CHRISTMAS

George Ayoub

iUniverse, Inc.
New York Lincoln Shanghai

Warm, for Christmas

iUniverse, Inc.

For information address:
iUniverse, Inc.
2021 Pine Lake Road, Suite 100
Lincoln, NE 68512
www.iuniverse.com

ISBN: 0-595-32776-1 (pbk)
ISBN: 0-595-66684-1 (cloth)

Printed in the United States of America

For Max

Contents

CHAPTER 1

Life, Death, and Holiday Music

"Great! Just what I need. Another Christmas. Another rotten Christmas."

Ridgeway was handing out Christmas songs in October, and I was thinking about skipping the whole deal. Thanksgiving, too, and New Year's if it's going to be mushy.

Ridgeway was Arthur Ridgeway, Salton Elementary's beefy, bearded music teacher, given to fits of anger if he caught you trading gossip in the back row or smirking during somebody's solo. A fifth-grade boy revealed as a snickering sinner in vocal music would darken Ridegway's perpetually red face, "the badge" my Aunt Merlene said, she being a self-appointed knower of all things.

"The man's a drinker," she would sniff. "I can see it in his face." This from a woman whose sister married into the Kavanagh clan, as good an Irish drinking family as you could find in Traynor.

"Sean, is there a problem?" Mr. Ridgeway asked, his glare more menacing, his whole being transforming into a dyspeptic basso profundo.

"Problem?"—I wanted to say—"of course there's a problem. My mother died three years ago, eaten from the inside by cancer in a world of evil details no eight-year-old should ever have to know. Since then my family has fallen apart, especially at Christmas. My old man hasn't stopped working since the funeral, my oldest brother is a perpetual know-it-all no-show, and my other brother couldn't pass a UA if his life depended on it."

And nobody knew that by Christmas his life would depend on it.

"Sean?"

"No, no problem, Mr. Ridgeway," I said, my face flush, my body damp with embarrassment.

"Then pass the music along," he boomed, his failed baritone filling the stage and echoing across the gray linoleum in the gym, which at Salton was gymnasium, cafeteria, auditorium, and site of the spring carnival, a festival of sugar ingestion and overwrought parents spending money, so the school could buy shiny slides and basketball hoops and dodge balls without bothering the taxpayers any further.

❧   ❧   ❧

If I'm going to tell you this story, I'd better introduce everyone. My name is Sean Kavanagh, but everybody called me Pachy then—except Ridgeway and Mrs. Ploutz, the principal, a cheerless woman about as happy as rain on the last day of school.

Mom christened me Pachy because of the elephantine stumps I had for legs as a baby, the kind you would find on Dumbo. By kindergarten I had outgrown the Michelin Man look, but Pachy stuck like a small town reputation. I loved to crawl into Mom's lap and have her tell me the story. "Well, honey, when you were only a few days old…" she would start, her eyes the pale blue of a high sky in April darting about as she spun a wondrous tale of chubby legs and how I became her little Pachyderm. I asked her once at the end, when the morphine was thin and her gasps were staccato, a terrible rat-a-tat-tat. I asked her to tell me one more time. She did. That was the last time.

My dad is John Kavanagh of Kavanagh and Sons Contractors. That's because Grandpa Jack started the company and because after Mom died, work—building houses and offices and strip malls—was about all my father ever did. When Mom was alive he was sort of an assistant parent anyway, but at least he was there. Now, he was usually gone in the morning and home late for dinner, which Mrs. Pilcher made for us after Mom came home for the last time from the cancer center. Dad told me work was all about our college funds and food on the table, but John Kavanagh of Kavanagh and Sons Contractors was hiding something.

Patrick is my oldest brother, tall with wispy hair the color of an October sunset and a face too young for graduate school—even with the tortoise shell glasses. He was 23 when Ridgeway passed out Christmas music in October to my fifth grade, and he preferred Kierkegaard to baseball, a shortcoming I've never understood even if his master's degree was going to be in philosophy, a major my father said would land him a job at a shoe store.

That's good because Patrick wore Birkenstocks and looked down on those who didn't. He once brought home a girl who called herself a feminist, but her name was Wanda, a name I'd never heard and resisted the temptation to laugh out loud at. That night, over some take out Mongolian beef and princess chicken in our kitchen, Patrick said Wanda was studying to be a midwife.

"A what?" I asked in a tone that brought a look from my father, scanning plans for the Phelps' new addition and nursing a Miller Lite.

"A midwife helps women have babies, Pachy," Wanda said, her voice low and raspy, her chop sticks moving at fork speed.

"Well, what's a feminist?" I insisted.

I never got the answer. Patrick was handing Wanda a large glass of water from the other side of the table. As Wanda extended her tan arm from her faded black sleeveless blouse, she revealed an awful two-inch shock of black hair where her arm met her shoulder. I froze, never having seen a man's armpit on a woman. I ran from the room with a yelp, sure that I was going to perish either from Wanda's worldliness at our kitchen table or from my father's response to my reaction to it.

Michael was 17 then, skinny with an unkempt pile of Dad's black hair and face designed by stoics. He was a supposed senior in high school but lurching nowhere in fits and starts. Mom's death had jumped his recreational marijuana use into a habit he rounded off the edges of with Budweiser or cheap wine. It was tough going for Michael, though. It's hard to let your drug abuse blossom on the salary of a part-time stock boy at the 7-Eleven.

Methamphetamine was Michael's next preferred stop—a couple of years later—but it took him a semester of four F's and a D to acquire a system that worked. He was usually just too damned stoned to make a connection—or do anything like have a conversation or drive me to football practice or look you in the eye.

Excuse my language. When I was a kid, Mom used to let me have a cussing session when something bad happened. Like when we lost the last coach pitch game, even though we weren't supposed to be keeping score. She and I went to my room, where I spewed and sputtered an awkward parade of four-letter entries (f-bombs were off limits) through tears and sweat and dirt. The two of us ended up holding close and giggling on my bed. I was eight and she was very sick. "Just a little tired, Sweetie," she'd say. I used to imagine what cancer looked like, and how it could have ever come to be part of something called my mother's ovaries.

If I close my eyes and concentrate, I can still smell her, her Shalimar and her powders and her Altoids. When she would have to go to the hospital or cancer center, I would spend hours in her room, sleeping on her pillow and smelling her clothes. Like a surgeon, I used to gently but purposefully touch her locked treasure box, which she allowed us to look inside, but only when she was with us. Now I know why.

I kept a half tin of her Altoids at the bottom of my sock drawer for seven years. They were the last ones she ever used to peppermint her breath. I lost them after I left for college and Dad sold the house and moved into a condo on Rose Street near the park.

Michael was a loser, but not like losing in baseball, and that Christmas he really ticked me off.

I was already mad because it was pretty much left up to me to get these three through another momless holiday. That's a heavy burden for a kid who was getting his parenting and relationship advice from such notable therapists as Scooby Doo and Punky Brewster.

❦   ❦   ❦

It was October but Ridgeway was already gearing up for his big night, the annual Salton Elementary Christmas Show, where he trotted out six grade levels of lungs wishing every doting parent and grandparent, every bratty younger sibling, and every surly older one a Merry Christmas.

I had a love/hate relationship with vocal music. Singing was a joy, at least that's what Mom said, but she never had Ridgeway's class where he insisted with all his girth and ferocity that we boys labor in the upper ranges. For those of us who, like Wanda, had sprouted a couple hairs under our arms the previous summer, this was not only physically excruciating, it was a falsetto blow to our blossoming manhood.

"All right, let's look at *O Little Town of Bethlehem*," Ridgeway said.

I was already gone. Hearing Ploutz call my name on the intercom. Listening to the snickers of the idiots who thought the Kavanaghs were weird. Hearing my dad stumble around for an explanation. Watching Michael's face for some sign of life.

"Sean Kavanagh, either pay attention or leave."

I was already gone.

Out the field of windows that was the west wall of Salton's vocal music room, I could see a police car pulling to the curb, followed by my father's white Ford F-150 pickup. A familiar figure hunched in the back of the patrol car. I couldn't see his eyes, but I knew the look. It was always the same: vacant, staring, nothing.

My dad got out and trudged up the sidewalk, festooned on either side with an orange and black riot of impending Halloween. He limped slightly, a tribute to a tumble off Bertie Sanders' roof just before Mom died. The cold exaggerated the limp, but Indian summer had blossomed in mid-September and blazed steadily for the last four weeks. Still, even in the warm afternoon he limped, eyes down, looking old and defeated.

In the back row where budding tenors were being forced to sing alto, I closed my eyes, squeezing hard to dam the water and trying not to imagine the handcuffs once again on Michael's wrists.

CHAPTER 2

A Decision for Michael

Aunt Merlene was waiting for us, a pot of weak coffee and the nascent trappings of a dinner in a haphazard jumble on the counter. She had dismissed Mrs. Pilcher for the day, deciding, as was (and still is) her wont to do, to steer this ship herself, to put this fire out the way only Merlene Jakobowski could.

The questions and accusations started when Dad, Michael, and I were still 10 feet from the back door. We Kavanagh men fought back: a series of grunts amid a tapestry of long silences, none of which deterred her chirping.

And her questions: What happened? Why? How could you, Michael? She was Mom's oldest sister, born a generation too late and mother to the entire world, especially the Kavanaghs. Her tombstone should read, "Here lies Aunt Merlene. Take a sweater. You'll catch a chill."

Mom's other sister is my Aunt Beth, who, like Mom, is quiet. I always figured Mom and Aunt Beth probably wanted to talk when they were growing up, but Aunt Merlene never left any time for them. So they just became quiet.

Aunt Beth is five years younger than Mom and lives in Michigan. She used to come for Christmas and for a week in the summer. She and Uncle Don don't have kids, a fact Aunt Merlene has never let go.

❦   ❦   ❦

The walk from the music room to the office seemed longer than the Iditarod and a little colder, even in the afternoon heat. After watching Dad move up the sidewalk, I realized that most of my music class was staring too. Soon, a chorus of whispers rose as I started fussing with my backpack. Ridgeway sensed discord.

"Quiet, class! Sean, what do you think you're doing?"

"I need to go to the office."

"Says who?" he thundered. Before he could finish the rebuke, Mrs. Rombaugh, Ploutz's secretary, mercifully interrupted.

"Mr. Ridgeway?"

"Yes?"

"Is Sean Kavanagh in class?"

"Yes."

"Please have him bring his things and come to the office." She might as well have added, "You see his brother is a drug freak and currently occupying the back seat of Officer Logan's cruiser," because everybody in Ridgeway's fifth-grade vocal music class knew that—all of it.

"Fine," said Ridgeway. He turned his massive frame and contemplated the scene outside his windows. He surveyed the black-and-white and the pickup with Kavanagh and Sons Contractors on the side. He turned back and looked directly at me, his face a bitter stew of pity and scorn. My Dad told me later I imagined it, but I know Ridgeway, and he sneered, a slight curl of his lip evident through his beard. I was already awash in embarrassment, and now, as I faced him, sweat oozed from my forehead.

"You'd better go, Mr. Kavanagh," Ridgeway said, looking away.

"Hey, Pachy," whispered Leon "Buddy" Bridges IV as I shuffled past a row of boys to the end of the metal riser. "You want my dad's card?"

This brought snorting and coughing from the squeaky alto boys two deep on either side of Buddy, whose dad was a lawyer raising, in my humble estimation, the next king of the village idiots.

I hopped down from the riser and walked toward the door, which seemed a good 12 miles across the room. My backpack effected a rakish nonchalance in an attempt to quell the growing attention to my plight. I had learned that a little swagger could disarm the anticipation that a boy might actually cry in front of Buddy and his stupid friends. My shirt stuck to my back where 62 eyes bore into me, now only a few steps from the safety of the shiny, empty hallway. With only a few feet to go, I considered going back and punching Buddy's lights out, earning detention until I was a junior in college and a lifelong grounding from John Kavanagh; or I could leave and suffer the indignities roiling behind my back.

This was no easy choice. I once punched Jordan McCumber for saying my mom was skinny. Dad said Jordan knew nothing about cancer, but we did, and that's all that counted. Such insight included grounding me from TV for two weeks. Double jeopardy being in vogue at my house, I also spent a Ploutz-assigned week in detention at school. Both stretches were worth it, as was the scratchy red blotch Jordan wore on his cheek for a few days.

I walked out of music, never looking back, leaving Buddy and Ridgeway and everyone else in Bethlehem.

❦   ❦   ❦

The office was humane, brief, with nods and murmurs between Dad and Ploutz. We walked in silence to the Ford, the eyes of Ridgeway's class and every other class on the west side of the building reboring holes in my already scarred back.

"Where we going?" I snapped, getting in.

"We're going to follow that police car because your brother is in the back seat."

We moved slowly. "Is he busted? Is he going to jail again?" Michael had spent a few hours in the pokey the year before, and had to pay a fine for loitering. The police thought he was selling dope, having no idea of his genuine lack of enterprise.

"No, he's going to the station to meet with a detective. Then we're taking him home." He stared straight ahead, Michael's head bobbing in the car in front of him.

"Then why's he in handcuffs? And why did the cop car have to come to school?" I demanded.

"Let's just talk about it later, Pachy," Dad said, employing the old Kavanagh dodge. "Are you okay?"

"Why did you come and get me at school, and with the cop car? Everybody could see it." My voice had jumped into an octave Ridgeway would approve of.

Dad sighed heavily. "School was about out and I didn't have time to make two trips. The officer would have just taken Michael, but he wanted to see if you could come with us now. I have to be there when the detective talks to him."

"Where was he?" I knew the answer.

"Michael?"

"Yeah, where was he when the cops got him?"

"On Prospect, with his doper buddies." Prospect Street was where new Traynor morphed into old Traynor, a jagged few blocks of liquor stores, bars, convenience stores, and empty lots that filled with Traynor's finest flotsam most nights. Downtown, with two new office buildings, the 12-plex, and the civic center, was only two streets over, a different world of business suits and real linen for lunch, where most everybody had their teeth as far as I could tell. A block the other direction was Oaklawn, a neighborhood whose rambling, old wooden houses were being bought and gentrified by young couples with minivans and professors from Farmington College.

There were only three reasons for a kid to hang out on Prospect. The first two were trouble; the third was to coax somebody off of it. Dad made the trip often. Michael was a drugstore junkie, but Prospect stretched cold, gray and mean in both directions. He was too soft to be a fixture on Prospect. Dad knew that. After Michael came home bloodied a few times, he and Dad had an understanding about rides.

Forty-five minutes later, we left the police station. The detective had talked to Michael and then, in the hallway, to Dad in whispers punctuated with glances at Michael and a couple at me. Michael slumped on the bench next to me, smelling like Prospect Street. I read my social studies book, wondering what life was like in Madagascar and Mozambique.

Still, I leaned far enough over a map of Africa to pick up a snippet or two: "School...required...bad people...recovery...too much money...no choice."

We rode home in gloom, the sadness etched on Dad's face, now older than when he left home that morning. Michael stared ahead, until, oddly, he and Dad made small talk about the unusual heat. "Great," I thought. "We're unraveling. Michael's a small-time criminal, Christmas is coming, nobody ever mentions Mom anymore, and the best you can do is talk about the weather."

❧   ❧   ❧

Aunt Merlene continued her onslaught about goals and the future and embarrassment and all the things he had been given. Michael sat crumpled at the kitchen table. I fended her off with my social studies book in front of my face at the counter.

As she moved into a new key, she accompanied the rant with the banging of pots and pans, the crescendo of which I was hoping would be goulash. Aunt Merlene is a little loony, but her goulash is a wonder.

Then, like a mysterious bang in the night, she stopped even herself. "Michael, what would your poor mother think?" I put my book down. An eerie quiet stilled us. Michael turned to Aunt Merlene, his eyes watery, either from weeping or some combination of uppers and downers or some cause and effect thereof.

"I'm going to treatment," he said in a small, hollow voice, the words starting somewhere deep inside him and not quite making the entire journey to his lips. "The cops are making me, but I'm going. Leave Mom out of this."

Dad, in a tone I'd not heard for some time, said, "Merlene, nobody feels like talking." Then he started for his office above the garage, hoping to hole up with the Phelps' plans until she left. Before he made it halfway across the kitchen, Aunt Merlene burst into tears. He stayed, to help set the table.

She cried over the goulash, which we ate in silence. She drank coffee and watched us and cried some more. She did the dishes and offered to take me to football practice, a proposal trumped by Dad. She dragged a wash rag across the counter, kissed Michael and me on the head with a perfunctory nod, and stomped out the door.

"Michael's going to be gone for a while, Pachy," Dad said as he drove me to practice.

"I know."

"This time it's going to be a little different." Michael had been to rehab twice and actually stayed clean a few months after the second stint. He used about 12 hours after leaving the first time.

"No, it won't be, Dad."

"Yes, he's going to Astoria to a locked ward for 60 days. He should be home for Christmas. This time it will be different."

"I don't think so."

"It's longer and tougher."

"He'll stay clean there. But sooner or later, he'll have to come home, Dad."

We drove the rest of the way in mutual silence.

CHAPTER 3

The Truth, Almost, and a Gift

We won our football game Saturday, two days after the cops brought Michael to school and nearly ruined what was left of my fifth-grade life, and one day after Dad called the Wicks Treatment Center in Astoria and was told an antiseptic room was ready for Michael.

What Dad deftly omitted from his this-time-it-would-be-different-for-Michael sales pitch as we drove to practice Thursday was the either-or corollary: Either Michael showed up at Wicks and stayed put for 60 days or he would be looking at jail time. Seems enough dope was in his pocket to reduce his choices to two.

I discovered this little unhappy detail five days after Michael left. Aunt Merlene had barged in on a warm Wednesday, asking about Michael and, like a loaded carbine, firing "what she had heard." We were in the kitchen, the venue for all great Kavanagh epiphanies and family fights.

"So it's true, John, Michael was going to jail?" Aunt Merlene queried as I scanned the refrigerator for food. Dad looked at Aunt

Merlene and then back at me, a wounded wince gathering at the corners of his eyes as if pain was either arriving or leaving.

"Well, kinda," he hedged.

"What?" I demanded, throwing daggers with my pale blues at John Kavanagh, my right hand still holding the fridge door open.

"Close the door, Pachy," Aunt Merlene said, able to tell me what to do and argue with my father all in the same moment, a multi-tasking meddler. "Martha McClusky said her brother-in-law told her as much. And he's a police clerk at the station, so he ought to know, all the paperwork and details and all," she said, her eyes widening, her voice on breath deficiency. Martha McClusky was the matriarch of the Motor Mouth McCluskys, Traynor's busiest bodies. If a rumor needed started, spread, or detailed, you called a McClusky.

Looking back, I suppose Aunt Merlene had apprenticed with her. But at the time, I was too angry to consider her development as a buttinski.

"You never said anything about that," I dared my father.

He ignored my challenge, instead locking and loading for a battle with his sister-in-law. "Michael told you, Merlene, that the police were making him go to treatment. What did you think he meant?"

"Dad, why didn't…"

"Be quiet, Pachy. Your aunt needs to mind her own business." His eyes narrowed.

"Mind my own business!" she shouted, tilting her head and looking at the kitchen ceiling. "Mind my own business. Since Clare died, who has cooked and cared and cleaned up your messes, John? Who has worried herself sick about Michael? Who has paid attention to Pachy when you've worked day and night?" My eyes burned. I could hear myself breathing.

"Nobody asked you to."

"Sure you did, John. You asked when you said, 'I do.' When you made a life with Clare, you made a life with her family. Don't you see?"

Dad waited, drawing a breath, his spare frame puffed at the chest. "I need you to stay out of this, Merlene, just this once."

"Can't. Too far in. Too much love has gone around."

"Merlene, stop it!" Now Dad was shouting.

"What did he do, John?…He had to have done something. They don't just ask you to leave town for loitering on Prospect with those other druggie idiots." Tears brimmed at the edges of Aunt Merlene's eyes. "Thank God, Clare isn't here to see this."

The sound slowly crawled upward from an untapped well, a place deep within me, one I never knew existed. The sound surfaced, exploding in a scream, a blast, an acrid, mushrooming "No!" which roared through the kitchen like a backdraft accelerated by a reservoir of pain.

"No!" I convulsed again, screaming with such force that my throat ached and my jaws throbbed. "No!" I shuddered, more quiet now, my father and aunt staring at me.

"No, no, no, no," I stammered, small explosions themselves. "No," I spit. "Mom should be here. She'd make it right. She'd fix Michael. She'd know what to do. If God wanted us to be okay, she would never have got cancer."

My outburst rang in my ears; the kitchen was shrouded in funeral home silence. I blinked away the tears. "I've got homework," I said and headed for my room, leaving Aunt Merlene and Dad to stare at their shuffling feet.

Aunt Merlene was first, about 15 minutes later. Dad showed up when I was nearly asleep. I said all the right things. Made them feel better. I was good at that. Told them everything would be okay.

I wasn't buying it.

❧   ❧   ❧

What I got from Dad the next day at breakfast was that Michael's pocket problems were not the first and that only some intervention by Grandpa Jack had kept my brother out of jail before.

Grandpa Jack, with his perfect white hair and gnarled fingers, lived in Florida with Audrey, his second wife, who wore too much makeup and was employed full-time spending Grandpa Jack's money. My grandmother, Gramps' first wife, Lucille, died in a car crash on Paducah Parkway before I was born, leaving her to my imagination and faded pictures in photo albums. She never really looked happy in any of the snapshots, but then she was married to Grandpa Jack, who worked until the late news and drank Bushmills when he didn't.

A run of good fortune and some government contracts made Grandpa Jack a wealthy man by Traynor standards. After Lucille ran a stop sign and was crushed under the weight of a Peterbilt full of frozen seafood, Grandpa Jack, with a rather gruesome irony, stopped working and took up golf.

Dad and Uncle Mick ran the company; Gramps bought some Pings and three months later met Audrey, who worked at the Salton Country Club as a hostess. They made a minor spectacle of themselves for a time, then moved to Fort Lauderdale, from where a postcard arrived one day pronouncing them man and wife.

But Grandpa Jack still had friends in high places in Traynor, and he used them to rescue his grandson on a couple of occasions. He apparently had at least one marker left in the fall of 1986, one he had Dad play for Michael.

"The police, well, Joe Detering, said if Michael would do 60 days at Wicks, they would look the other way. But Joe said it would be for the last time." Dad was filling in the blanks over coffee while I pushed a couple pieces of bacon around my plate.

Joe Detering went to high school with Dad and was always considered a friend in our house. He brought Michael home the first time from Prospect, mortifying Dad.

"Can Joe do that?" I dug a little.

"Well, he did and there's no way we can repay him except with our respect, Pachy."

I chased a pull of bacon with some juice and wondered how we did that.

❧   ❧   ❧

Dad and Michael missed the game, the last of our season of five, because they were on their way to Wicks, where Dad thought the world was going to change and where I knew at least someone else would have to worry about my brother for a couple months. I wasn't glad he was gone, but fall suddenly became less complicated. Or so I thought.

Missing my game was really no big deal anyway. Michael had never shown up; Patrick came for one but it was an afterthought of a rare weekend at home. Dad made them all but never for the whole game, the pull of work and the accessibility of the pickup just too great.

I played football because Jackson Fowler did. He lived across the street and was the closest thing I had to a best friend. He was a real jock, unlike me who knew the rules and did enough to get by. Fifth grade was my first foray into tackle football, where I graded out about B minus. Aunt Merlene said I was going to get hurt, and Dad said I was too good-natured to want to smack somebody.

I accumulated the normal bumps and bruises of an outside linebacker, where my job was to throw ball carriers to the earth and be ferocious about it. This I did with infrequent expertise during a two-wins, three-losses campaign plagued by fumbles, fifth-grade focus, and mornings too summery for October.

Our coach, Ronnie Brazille, played tight end at Farmington and is rumored to have had a tryout with the Steelers, although no amount of research could verify it, and we were all afraid to ask lest he believe we were doubting his résumé. Extra windsprints would be sure to follow.

So I stumbled through practice and games, a fair to middling linebacker, with a wacko family, a dead mom, and limited skills. After Mom died, Mrs. Smith, the school counselor, told Dad I needed to go talk to somebody. That ended up being Dr. Ontiveras, who always wore a white smock and wanted to know if I had bad dreams. I went to her for a couple months but stopped, convincing Dad I was cured. He was spending all his energy keeping Michael in school and, as I came to find out, out of jail, so he agreed. Mrs. Smith had been after me to go back, a request I had deflected with football practice and football games.

I did think once during the season about Dr. Ontiveras, wondering if she could explain—she was awfully convincing about why I felt what I did even though I had no idea how I felt most of the time—what happened during a tackling drill a week into the season. Brazille was on us to drive through the ball carriers, and so, on his whistle, we tackled the poor slob who was next in line and then pounded our tired feet until we heard the succor of his shrill whistle. When I came to the front of the line, Joey Sindelar, all 125 pounds—30 more than me—sneered through his face mask.

Brazille "hutted" us into action. Suddenly I yelled, not like the explosion in my kitchen a month later but similar, without notice. I drove into Joey's paunchy belly and with inexplicable power lifted him off his feet as I jackhammered mine. Brazille blew the whistle, but I kept going, Joey screaming at me, Brazille watching his average linebacker out of control. Spent, I finally deposited Joey with a thud and me in a heap atop him. He groaned. Our face masks touched; he had tears in his eyes.

I turned away quickly because so did I.

❋   ❋   ❋

The Fowlers took me for a victory lunch at Ferguson's Tasty Treat and then home. On the way, I thought about what Michael meant when he said good-bye that morning.

"Hey, Pack Man," he said as he leaned against my door jamb. "Remember that song Mom used to sing to us, the Toola song."

"No," I lied.

"I was watching TV last night real late, flippin' the channels. I heard it. Some priest was singing it in some old movie. Weird, man. See ya."

"Yeah, see ya."

That was the best I could do.

"Hey, Pachy, there's a present on your porch," Jackson said. Sure enough, a small package, wrapped in shiny red paper with a yellow bow was on the top step of the porch.

We piled out of the AstroVan. I headed across the street, eyeing the package, wondering what was inside.

CHAPTER 4

A Happy Photo, Once

Mom died upstairs, in her bed where she used to read me stories. I was partial to *Pooh* and *Where the Wild Things Are,* but we read hundreds, or so it seemed, all intertwined against the pillows, the world racing by outside the window, but there, in her bed, the warm moments ambled along, lasting forever.

Mom was never in a hurry when she had you in a love grip or read you a good book or stroked your face with the back of her soft fingers.

I was watching television when she closed her eyes for the last time. I can't tell you what I was watching. I only stared at television and books and the sky that summer, just needing a break from looking at my mother's waxpaper skin or listening to her whispery gasps. I used to watch her sleep, hoping, in my best eight-year-old thinking, to see the cancer through her nearly translucent face. If I could see the cancer, we could get the doctor to grab it, and Mom would be up and singing songs at breakfast and scolding Michael about his hair and teasing Patrick about his uppity vocabulary and catching Dad with a kiss when he sauntered in for dinner. And she would hold me when the world was too scary or too big or too unruly for a kid.

Dad or Aunt Merlene or somebody usually chased me out after a while, my eyes sore from squinting after diseases.

Clare Marie Kavanagh left on a Sunday afternoon, August 7, 1983. Dad came to the top of the stairs but didn't need to come down. The penetrating silence from upstairs issued a new clarity, as if two silences were meshing into one. I leaped from the chair and raced around the corner to the foot of the stairs. Dad was at the landing, the door to their room open, the sun backlighting him, silhouetting his face, and hiding the deep circles of grief and exhaustion.

"Pachy," he started.

"Did she say anything?" I asked.

"She was quiet and very peaceful. She sure loved you, Pachy," he said, swallowing hard. I never saw him cry about Mom, from the time she came home from the doctor's office with cancer clear through her funeral, when everyone cried, even after three years to get ready not to. John Kavanagh's youngest didn't cry much after the funeral either.

I ran upstairs, pausing in front of Dad. He put a hand on my shoulder, Kavanagh manspeak for a hug and a kiss. I walked toward the bedroom. I had never seen a dead person, but then I was only eight.

Mom looked asleep, her head with a funny tilt against her pillow. I thought her mouth was almost making a smile, but maybe I was just hoping it would. Michael and Patrick were in the room; Patrick, arms crossed in a dare, looking out the window, which was streaming warm light. Michael was in the big, navy blue chair at the foot of the bed, his elbows on his knees. He rocked aimlessly back and forth, heel, toe, heel, toe. His chin quivered. Aunt Merlene swept past me in the doorway, then shooed us out. I lingered a moment.

I would touch Mom's cheek at the funeral home, gentle like she used to touch mine. I didn't realize it, but it was my good-bye in the physical sense.

Patrick and Michael left the room walking past me. I think Patrick was crying. I followed but both of them disappeared into their rooms, so I went back downstairs and watched TV.

Second grade started 22 days later. Dad took a week off work. Patrick hung around home for four days. Michael stayed in his room all the time. Aunt Merlene was there every day. The rest of my life had changed forever.

※   ※   ※

I sat on Mom's bed with the surprise package, the glossy red paper shimmering from the ceiling fan's whirl. Dad hadn't done much to change the room, so it still had plenty of Mom in it, including the fan.

She used to say that you should savor each gift in your life, milk the mystery. We usually ignored her, tearing into Christmas and birthday packages with a material feeding frenzy. She didn't mean wrapping paper and bows, but I was just a kid so what did I know.

That day, alone in the house, now quieted by Michael's trip to Wicks with Dad behind the wheel, I decided to savor like Mom.

❦   ❦   ❦

Father Salem hurried her funeral, obviously unaware that Mom wouldn't want it that way. Afterward, when everyone came to our house and ate Aunt Merlene's goulash and Martha McClusky's sandwiches, I heard people thank him for his brief but stirring service, surely grateful that their discomfort in a place of grief was shortened.

Father Salem was a short man, with a wry smile; his family came from Lebanon, where they were strict Maronite Catholics. He was pastor at St. Mary's when Mom got sick, and he visited her often. He usually skipped the small talk, preferring instead to get to the point or go right to the big questions of life and death and church attendance. No wonder she was tired when he left.

I kept my distance from St. Mary's spiritual leader, my well-documented catechism truancies and church hookeys being sins too great to overcome, a sure ride to hell or a lengthy conversation with Salem the Slammer.

❦   ❦   ❦

I turned the package over in my hands, feeling its shape, rectangular with pointed edges, and some weight to it, too. It was about the size of the music holder on Ridgeway's electric piano.

In a perfect fold I found an imperfect ledge, too much paper where less should be. I fidgeted with the flaw, hoping to smooth it completely before I solved the glistening mystery with the pretty yellow bow. A couple surgical tugs of the wrapping paper exposed a white edge, thicker than the paper. I squeezed it between two dirty fingernails and pulled. A card fell from the gift, landing on the bed ink down.

I turned it over. "To Pachy. Open before Christmas. With love."

That was it. "With love" who? I wondered. No name, no initials, no nothing. The savoring complete, I tore into the red paper, shredding like a guilty office worker. Inside the crimson exterior, layers of tissue paper shrouded my prize. My hands found cool glass. I flung the last tissue aside.

A smiling family stared at me in four-color relief, Lake Anastasia and a greened, medium size mountain, a member of the Sable Range, behind, comely testaments to prehistoric volcanoes. Five smiles beamed at me, not grins posed and coaxed by a professional photographer, but five spontaneous eruptions of happiness.

Mom had me in her lap, Patrick and Michael sat proudly on John Kavanagh's knees. We wore the clothes of happiness, too—fishing gear and swimming suits and floppy hats. Cares and cancer were somewhere behind the camera, miles from the f-stop of this moment, years after Lake Anastasia and the warmth of the summer and wholeness of the Kavanaghs.

I touched each face, slowly, as if not to erase them accidentally. I ran my fingers over the burgundy frame, its finish smoothed from routers and sanders and varnish. I turned the picture over and over, looking at it from every conceivable angle, looking for some clue, some hint, some suggestion of how this happy family came to be leaning against the pillar on my front porch.

❀   ❀   ❀

"What happens if he doesn't stay all 60 days?" I pumped Dad for information.

We were working our way through an Aunt Merlene-preheat-to-350-cook-for-30-minutes-uncover-and-cook-another-10 casserole. I had no idea what it was, but hunger made it delicious. Dad got home about 7 p.m. from Wicks and a stop at his office where he fretted for an hour over straight lumber and truculent plumbers. He called, so I threw the casserole in the oven per Aunt Merlene's instructions. Now he was working on a cold Miller Lite, a hot meal, and changing the subject.

"Did Patrick call?" he asked, his face never rising from the plate.

"No. Does he know? Are you going to call him? You want me to?"

"No, Pack, I'll do it."

"When?"

"I don't know. Why?"

"He should know. He's his brother."

"Michael hasn't died, Pachy. He's in treatment."

"Well, he's killing the rest of this family," I said, knowing I'd gone too far, said too much. "Sorry," I offered.

Dad sighed, his signature emotion for the last three years.

"So what will happen? If he runs away, will he go to jail?"

"I don't know. I don't know. Look, Pachy, I'm really tired. I just want to eat and then go to bed. Okay?"

"Sure," I said. We finished in silence. I put my dishes in the sink and headed to the TV room.

"Yes," said my father behind me.

"Huh?" I kept my back to him.

"Michael will go to jail if he runs away or even leaves. He'll go to jail for a long time."

"Oh." I let the two blasts of new reality sink in. My father had come clean, and my brother was one more stupid decision from being a jailbird. That ought to play well at Salton Elementary. "Thanks, Dad."

I turned around. He nodded, pushed his plate away, and slumped in silence at the kitchen table.

CHAPTER 5

Buddy Pays the Mooch

I walked with Jackson to school Monday. He was waiting for me on the sidewalk, his red and yellow backpack slung over his left arm and cradled at the shoulder. He was bouncing a basketball with his right hand. Football season ended Saturday, so Jackson was getting ready for basketball, a sport I avoided like a good-bye kiss from Mrs. Pilcher.

Dad had left an hour earlier, the warm and sunny fall turning winter construction finishes into Thanksgiving ones. He told Mrs. Pilcher, who got there at 6 a.m. to fix us breakfast and start on her housekeeping chores, that he would be late. I had cereal and juice in silence while Mrs. Pilcher carried on a conversation with a morning news show, her slight German accent enough to mangle the weatherman's last name.

Grandpa Jack called her a war bride. When Mom was near the end, Mrs. Pilcher just showed up one day to cook and clean. She was a widow who lived in the retirement apartments on Grandview and heard about Clare Kavanagh's cancer at St. Mary's during prayers of the faithful. Mrs. Pilcher was a fixture at daily Mass.

She made us breakfast and worked until Art Fosskey and his wife, Ethyl, picked her up at exactly 8:50 every weekday for church at St. Mary's. She came back and stayed until dinner was ready to put in the oven.

Dad, self-conscious of this stranger's generosity, hired her the week after the funeral. She kept her distance but twice grabbed me for a grandmotherly smooch as I left. After the second time, I planned a better escape route.

"Hey," Jackson said, dribbling with a confident nonchalance.

"Hey."

"So what was the present?"

"What present?" I lied. "Oh, the one on the porch. Yeah. It was for my dad," I lied again. I had been doing that a lot lately.

"What was it?"

"Some old thing from somebody he built a house for."

"But what was it?"

"I didn't ask." The second lie is usually easier. The third one is a snap.

❄   ❄   ❄

Buddy Bridges and a passel of nitwits spied me from the steps and launched a volley of sneers in my direction. He knew better than to bust my chops when Jackson was around. Jackson Fowler was big and tough and probably wouldn't think twice about intervening with a left hook or a right cross if Buddy was a jerk. This kept Buddy at bay that morning, at least until recess when Jackson's class left the playground as mine emerged.

I ambled toward the benches near the gym, looking for Brian "Moochie" Clark, another pal who claimed he went to dirty movies and once ate an entire bottle of ketchup. He was goofy and his stories always unconfirmed, but I liked the guy anyway.

"Hey, Mooch," I yelled. He was already on the bench, punishment for throwing a dodge ball in the face of the perpetually fragile Margaret Fletcher last week. While she went wailing to the nurse, Moochie pleaded his case (an accident) with the omnipresent Ploutz, who had swooped down on the crime scene with talons bared. A week-long benching was not uncommon, but this was Moochie's second and November was only five days away.

"Hi, Pack. Heard about Michael." His voice was squeaky, his head aflame in orange curls and his face two dimples from a solid freckle. His 70 pounds was mostly hair and huge sneakers he hoped one day to grow into.

"Yeah." I sat down next to him. In a small town and among fifth graders, gossip speeds like the wind of a sudden storm.

"How long he gonna be there?"

"Sixty days."

"Your old man mad?"

"Not really. I think he's done being mad." I stared at the ground, not even wanting to make eye contact with a friend.

"Hey, Pack Rat, your dope fiend brother called. Wants you to break him out." I looked up. Buddy Bridges had found me, a brace of husky lackeys in tow, a smirk on his pointy face. Given the size of his escort—two greasy sixth graders I'd seen around but couldn't remember their names—I shifted uneasily on the bench, thinking Buddy might want to fight or at least slap me around a little.

"What's the matter, Pack Rat? Too drugged to talk?" I looked across the playground for a teacher as Buddy and his two pals pressed closer. "What's the matter, Pack Rat?" he taunted, now inches from my face.

"Shut up, Buddy boy." I jumped, afraid the words had come from my mouth. I looked right and Moochie was glaring at Buddy, burning holes right though him the way only a frustrated fifth grader, who has been benched for a week, could.

Buddy turned his attention to Moochie, then back to me. "You're nothing, Kavanagh."

"Gee, you're something, Buddy girl," Moochie said, burying me deeper into the bad side of big guys. "You think these guys make you tough, Robbie and Seth make you tough?"

"What do you want, Buddy?" the words finally formed in my parched throat.

"Nothing, Kavanagh. Just checking on your druggie brother," he sneered and turned to Moochie. "Clark, you've got a big mouth. Maybe we oughta shut it." Buddy reached out to tap Moochie on the cheek, but in an instant Moochie slapped his hand away. Buddy recoiled and clenched his fist. Robbie and Seth looked confused.

"Buddy, is everything okay?" Ploutz had a voice somewhere between sandpaper and a serrated edge. Still, I was relieved to see her.

"Yes, ma'am. We were just talking," Buddy lied.

"Brian is benched and Sean is going to be if he doesn't move along. You, too, Buddy, and Seth and Robbie, you should know better than to talk to benched students. You're sixth graders, for heaven's sake."

I took off, scanning the playground for adult security and steering clear of Buddy. The bell finally rang, freeing Moochie and protecting me from any further humiliation.

So I thought. Two days later in music, as Ridgeway was explaining the details of our role in the Christmas show, Buddy raised his hand and asked if drug addicts could come to the show, "if they are released for the holidays." I swallowed hard, knowing where he was going.

"That's an odd question, Buddy."

"Well, Pachy might need to know." The class erupted in shock and laughter. I burned, knowing my pale Irish skin had turned scarlet.

"Buddy, that was uncalled for," Ridgeway said, trying to calm the class now spasming. A lesser mortal, one whose father was not the school district attorney and prime benefactor for fund drives and class projects, would be in Ploutz's office. That's how I saw things. Sean Kavanagh would be there. Jackson Fowler would be there. Even Margaret Fletcher would be there. "Buddy. Apologize," Ridgeway boomed.

The room went silent. My ears were so hot they hurt. I felt sick to my stomach. We waited.

"Sorry, Pachy," Buddy oozed—not an ounce more or less than his usual insincere self.

Across the room, Moochie was writing furiously.

❦   ❦   ❦

Thursday was another warm day, T-shirts and shorts the school uniform. Halloween would be Friday, so a K-6 school was a couple feet off the ground to start with. In all the excitement, no one expected such vengeance, such justice.

After first scanning the horizon for Ploutz, I found Moochie at morning recess. As I got near the bench, he held up a hand, checked both directions, then reached into his backpack. Like a first-year mime student, he pulled out a crumpled piece of notebook paper and handed it to me. He rechecked both directions, then shooed me away with a flick of his skinny wrist.

I found an unused corner of the building to lean on as I read: "Pack, Buddy pays today. Stay out of the way but close enough to see."

Great, I thought. Moochie is going to do something, and Buddy will have his goons pound me.

I went back to Moochie to protest.

"Mooch, what are you going to do? Buddy will think it's me."

"It will be worth it."

"Mooch, those are sixth graders. I'll be dead meat."

"No problem, Pack. Got it covered."

❦   ❦   ❦

I never asked him how he pulled it off. I have some theories that center on accomplices and teachers turning the other way, but no proof. Moochie wasn't talking either, never copping to the fur or the epoxy. He stayed in the background, as did I, while payback unfolded.

We trouped back to class after recess. Mrs. Jacobson, "the Jake" behind her back, took about 10 minutes to read some announcements. Then she told us to get out our math books so we could finish our board work. Buddy's problem had been interrupted by recess, so after we settled, she asked him to come forward.

Nothing happened. We turned to Buddy, who, inexplicably, was somehow affixed to his desk. A ripple of laughter rose, crashing in a wave as Buddy struggled against the forces of apparent glue.

"Buddy?" the Jake asked.

"Some idiot glued my desk," Buddy blubbered, glaring at me but not exclusively. Good, I thought. I'm only a suspect among many. Buddy's bullying was an equal-opportunity malevolence among fifth graders and younger. I just happened to be in the soup this week.

Buddy ripped his shirt lunging forward, but never moved from the seat. I looked at Moochie only once during Buddy's ordeal. He was smiling.

Eventually, we had to leave the room and go to the library while Buddy had the janitor and his father, who was summoned, cut him out of his pants. While Buddy put on different clothes, his father could be heard ranting in Ploutz's office.

We heard he did that again on the phone just after lunch. Seems Buddy's chicken patty turned out to be stuffed with golden hair that looked exactly like the coat of Moochie's yellow Lab, Butch. A gagging Buddy left for the day, his mother taking him home this time.

Mooch had more. I didn't see it, but Max Tuttle, who was coming back from the orthodontist, told me Buddy's bike fell apart as his mom rolled it toward their station wagon with an ashen Buddy in the front seat.

"Fell apart?"

"Yeah. It just kind of went everywhere. It looked like somebody loosened every screw and bolt. She just piled in the parts and drove off. Real fast."

I walked home alone, planning to hand out candy rather than soap windows. I thought about Moochie. I had prayed for my mom to live and Michael to get clean and world peace and the Lakers to beat the Celtics. But I'd never prayed for another fifth grader.

"God," I asked, hedging my bets on praising vengeance, "go easy on Moochie."

CHAPTER 6

A Letter from Michael and Another Gift

I used to worry I would wake up and not remember what she looked like. I would punch the switch on the lamp next to my bed and light her picture on my night stand, the one Dad took before we went to Cindy Pfizer's wedding. I'd stare hard, committing to memory her flaxen hair, her white teeth, her lucent smile outlined in lipstick the color of Joey Sindelar's dad's Corvette convertible.

I'm leaning against her in my first blue blazer and my first tie, a bright red affair with small blue and yellow bugs. Her simple, elegant black dress frames me; her blue eyes radiate happiness.

You forget in increments, memory being what it is; you let go when you can, when you have found something to fill the awful chill of loss. I heard Mom tell Aunt Merlene once that faith was about letting go, not holding on, about giving up.

❦   ❦   ❦

Monday came, and school buzzed with details of smashing pumpkins and stupid costumes. Randy Canton had broken his arm trying to outrun an irate homeowner whose windows were being soaped. Randy fell over a row of low bushes, screamed in pain, and then begged for mercy as the middle-aged sprinter stood over him. After diagnosing the situation, he drove Randy to the hospital, where he called the police and Randy's parents in that order. Randy had to cough up names while Dr. Ferrarini wrapped his right arm in warm cloth that would become his cast. We begged to sign it Monday. Randy, sporting a scratch, which arced from his right eyebrow to his left sideburn, and a swollen, plum-colored left elbow, would have none of it. He moped through the day in pain, trying to avoid the trio of accomplices he had fingered in the ER at Traynor Community Hospital.

Halloween and Randy were enough to make Buddy's Friday demise a mere subplot to the big weekend. Buddy was slightly subdued Monday, sneering in my general direction but saying nothing the entire week. I figured he had moved on, looking for fresh meat on the bully boy market.

Moochie looked contented, now that he had paid for his crimes against Margaret Fletcher. And that Buddy had gotten his.

I had spent the weekend watching television, sleeping late, and eating junk food. Dad worked Saturday and Sunday because "75-degree days will not last forever." The house was quiet.

We went to the Brick Bar for steak Saturday night. Dad had a couple of beers over his T-bone; I had three Cokes over a cheeseburger. Wendall Stallmeyer, his breath reeking of 35 years of Camels and eight hours of tap beer, made a nuisance of himself for about a half an hour, but otherwise it was Dad and me and small talk, punctuated with long silences while we surveyed the restaurant or fiddled with our food.

"Can Michael write us letters, I mean, if he wants to?" I plunged ahead.

"Yeah," Dad said, his eyes fixed on his plate.

"Think he will?"

"I doubt it." Dad looked up, holding a steak knife in his right hand. Dad was never going to be father of the year, but when I was little I always felt safe because of his hands: big, fleshy mitts, strong enough to keep the world away and able to fix anything—bikes, toys, brothers. He could pound and turn and pry and yank and lift about anything with his hands. They could perform miracles on the job site, but when I was eight, I realized they could not defeat cancer.

Dad took a deep breath. I figured the talk was going to get larger. "Pachy, in a month or so, I'm not sure exactly when, Michael told me but I forget, in a month or so, Wicks has something called family week."

"What's that?"

"Well, you and Patrick and me, we would go to Wicks and talk to Michael about how we feel about his problem."

"That he's a drug addict and a loser?"

"Come on, Pack. He's trying to turn it around."

Right, I thought. The house is quiet, but no police cars are arriving at school with my brother in the back. People can't say they saw him on Prospect or whisper in class and point and look at me. Aunt Merlene and Dad can disagree about whatever, but

they don't have to yell at each other about Michael. Thanksgiving
will be small, but that's okay, and Christmas is coming up. The
only thing I wanted was for Michael to get an extended stay at
Wicks, one that didn't involve me.

"Patrick won't come."

"It's a long way off."

"Will Aunt Merlene go?"

"No, it's just for Michael's immediate family."

"I don't want to go."

"You might not have any choice. Besides, how would Michael
feel if you didn't show up, his little brother? You guys used to be
pals."

"Do I have to?"

"I don't know, Pachy…I don't know." Dad sighed heavily,
defeated by drug rehab like he was by drug addiction like he was
by cancer. Nothing was plumb in those worlds, nothing
responded to a level and a 10-penny nail. I looked at my father in
the haze and Saturday night chatter of the Brick Bar and realized
that. Mom dying and Michael's drugs and Patrick being so far
away, those things made me sad, sorry for myself. It had never
occurred to me that they made Dad sad, too, or that I should feel
sorry for him.

"Sorry, Dad," I said lowly, unsure whether he heard me.

❦   ❦   ❦

School bounced along for a couple weeks, the excitement of
Halloween giving way to the gray routine of November. Mrs.
Pilcher sent me out the door every morning and waited for me
every afternoon. The weather stayed warm, so Dad usually got

home after I had polished off my share of a Pilcher casserole and was stumbling though my homework in front of *Family Ties* or *The Cosby Show*. I promised Mom I would study hard and had the grades to prove I did, but I liked the company of television while I was waiting for Dad. Sometimes I shot baskets with Jackson before dinner and talked the aimless talk of fifth grade. Aunt Merlene was a constant and constantly Aunt Merlene, but she usually left before prime time.

Buddy Bridges' father talked to our class about a week after the glue, hair and bike fiasco, reminding us that the right thing to do would be to identify the perpetrators. Sure, I thought, come clean and let the man in the front of the room in his $500 suit and shiny shoes put us in jail, where his doofus son could come by and taunt us.

Us, of course, was Moochie and me. My eyes never left Mr. Bridges' face during the 20 minutes he presented his case to the Jake's fifth grade; I figured a knowing glance at Moochie no match for Leon the III's lawyering ways.

Mrs. Jacobson thanked Mr. Bridges, and we re-entered the social studies universe where land bridges and guys named Magellan kept me occupied, safely out of range of Buddy's own leers around the room. Moochie had said very little to me since Halloween, a slight I assumed was the necessary sacrifice for Buddy to eat Labrador hair. The execution of fifth-grade vengeance required a complete reordering of relationships. Being new to the game, I was on a steep learning curve, but I did know that Moochie had been a target of Buddy's bullying for a long time.

No voice was ever raised or lowered to take credit for the Halloween massacre, not in some emotional confession in front of the Jake's class nor in any of the 17 years since. To my knowledge, Moochie Clark, who now straightens bumpers and smoothes dents at Lew's Body and Fender Shop in Traynor, has kept his own counsel.

✤   ✤   ✤

Three weeks after Halloween, on a sunny Friday afternoon, Ploutz stuck her pointy face inside Mrs. Jacobson's room and motioned for me to follow her. The usual understated hysteria swept the room as I rose to leave.

"Bring your things, Sean."

Michael flashed through my mind. He had sent me a short letter a couple days earlier:

Dear Pack Man,

How's it hanging, little brother? This place is tough. They yell at you all the time and they shaved my head because I didn't clean my room good enough. I hate it, but I have to stay. Wish me luck, Pack Man. Did you ever figure out that Toola song Mom used to sing? It's been bugging me.

Michael

What had he done now? Gone crazy? Killed a doctor? Run away? He said he hated it.

I dutifully followed the principal past three classrooms. Near the office and without turning around, Ploutz said, "Sean, you need to see Mrs. Smith." She pointed to a door on her right and continued down the empty hallway. I had been imagining my brother burning down not just the Wicks Center but the entire city of Astoria. Dad and I would have to leave the state, move, and change our names.

"Thank you," I said, but by then the clicking of her shoes had receded in the distance.

Phyllis Smith was a syrupy anti-Ploutz, always ready with a hug and smile. She was tall and thin with coal black hair and very red lipstick. She would kneel to talk to kindergartners and other short people and sit us bigger kids down because she had a thing about looking you in the eye. I thought it was to get you to confess, but that sold Mrs. Smith a little short. She was Salton's only counselor. I knocked softly.

"Come in, Pachy." I wondered how she knew it was me.

I opened the door, half expecting the police and Dad and Aunt Merlene and the president of the United States, all gathered to explain and chronicle Michael's last fated days at Wicks. Instead, Mrs. Smith was leaning against her desk. She nearly lunged when I was inside, hugging me.

"I haven't talked to you in a while, Pachy Kavanagh. How are you?"

"Fine, thank you." She released me finally, which was when, out of the corner of my eye, I could tell someone else was in the room.

"Hello, Pachy." I knew the voice. I turned quickly to find Dr. Ontiveras sitting in a wooden chair in the corner behind me.

"Hi." I was trapped. I was doomed.

"Sit down, honey," Mrs. Smith said. This woman loved everybody. "Now that football has ended, Dr. Ontiveras and I think maybe you should start seeing her again. Not that anything is wrong, but you've been through a lot lately." ("A lot" was Smith-speak for Michael and drugs and Wicks.) "What do you think?"

"I'm feeling okay," I said with a shrug.

"You know, Pachy," Ontiveras said, "I really enjoyed talking to you, about your dreams and your mom."

"Really, I'm okay," I insisted.

That's how it went for 15 minutes: their coaxing and my being okay. I could have better spent the time beating my head against the wall, considering Smith and Ontiveras had ambushed me and then lured me back into therapy.

I went back to class even though only a couple minutes were left in school, insurance against the rumor mill racing to a white-hot grind. Jackson asked if I wanted to walk home together, but I lied about having to get a book at the library.

The sun was slipping low when I saw the two porch columns of my house. Pilcher would be mad that I was late, but I needed some time to think, some time to work up my anger against Smith and Ontiveras. None came. Only an odd sense of relief.

I trudged up the porch steps where I could see Pilcher at the kitchen counter. At the foot of the door was a small package, wrapped in shiny, red paper with a yellow bow and a card I could read from where I stood: "To Pachy. Open before Christmas. With love."

CHAPTER 7

Black and White Movies and a Jackson Rescue

"The correct response to a helping hand," Mom used to say, "is 'thank you.' No need to gush or grovel." And when you give "for fun and for free"—another Mom thing—you should expect nothing more in return.

So I suppose I should have thanked Dr. Ontiveras and Mrs. Smith. But when you're 11 and two adults gang up on you like well-dressed bullies with perfume and lipstick, saying thanks seems to be the wrong call.

Mom was big on mysteries, too. She and Aunt Merlene discussed them in the kitchen over coffee and some tasty treat in the making, a carrot cake or brownies or a pie. I'd sit at the counter and fiddle and futz over some gewgaw, listening to my mother and aunt sifting Catholic doctrine, and getting none of it. I had my own mysteries anyway, like why cottage cheese tasted so awful or why Tony Barth, my tablemate in morning kindergarten, ate his boogers. While not rising to the level of a Wedding at Cana, spending three hours next to a guy who is snacking constantly took a serious article of faith.

❦   ❦   ❦

I had bounded past Pilcher, who was chewing me out for my tardiness and saying good-bye in one fell German/English crescendo, and leaped onto my bed to examine the shiny package. It was smaller than the first but wrapped the exact same way. My fingers worked their way around a hard, rectangular surface. I reached under my bed and fished out a dusty canvas bag. Reaching in and groping around for a few seconds, I found gift No. 1. I had kept the card and now compared the two. They looked like photocopies.

I tore open the paper to find a movie video. The cover said, "*Going My Way* starring Bing Crosby."

"An old movie?" I thought. On the cover were black and white images of a priest and some boys dressed in old clothes. I had never heard of Crosby or the movie, and besides, we didn't even have a VCR. They were still a novelty in 1986 to some, my father included. He'd rather buy a new table saw. My anonymous secret Santa must not know me very well.

I heard the door of Dad's pickup slam. I threw the movie, the wrapping paper and the card in the bag, shoved it under my bed, and ran downstairs. The widening mystery would have to wait.

"Hey, Dad."

"Hey, Pack." He was unusually dirty; I figured it had been an excavating day, a basement perhaps. He mostly supervised other subcontractors and hammered a few nails. Some days he spent almost entirely in his pickup. Uncle Mick did the same, but he had a thing about finishing concrete, to a fault. Dad used to laugh that he knew he'd be doing Mick's work when he would see his brother's rubber boots on a job site.

"Digging today?"

"Yeah, we had a problem with a remodel, and I had to help Gus with a trench. We didn't have room to get the backhoe in there." I liked it when Dad talked work to me, as if I were a peer, an equal, someone who understood linear feet and the pitch of a roof, someone with a sense of proportion, someone with big strong hands.

He was leaning against the counter, waiting for the microwave to complete its own finish work on Pilcher's latest sensation.

"Mrs. Smith talk to you today?" he said, looking directly at me.

"Yeah. How'd you know about that?"

"How about Dr. Ontiveras?"

"Yeah, she was there, too. Dad?"

"Do you have an appointment to see her?"

"Tomorrow after school. Dad, did you tell them to do this?"

"No, Pachy, but when Mrs. Smith called and said she thought it was a good idea for you to see Dr. Ontiveras again, I agreed."

"Dad, I'm okay. I told them that."

"Pack, ain't none of us okay. I want you to see Dr. Ontiveras." The beep of the microwave shattered our silence. He took his plate and headed for the table.

I said to his back, "Who you gonna talk to?" He turned and sighed, not angry, not defeated, just tired from digging trenches with Gus and burying his wife and trying not to bury his son.

"I wish I knew, Pachy. In the meantime, you see Dr. Ontiveras."

❦   ❦   ❦

The next day, Aracely Ontiveras was waiting for me after school in the extra room near Mrs. Smith's office. I haven't told you, but Ontiveras made me nervous because, besides my mom, she was the most beautiful woman I had ever seen. She was like a movie star. It was hard for me to look at her without blushing. Her black curly hair fell aimlessly over her shoulders. Her brown eyes looked like expensive mahogany, her pale sienna skin like it had been painted on.

I had always seen her at her office before, but today at school she had shed the white lab coat and looked like a regular movie star. She made arrangements with Smith to meet me at school as a convenience for me.

So now, for an hour, I had nothing to say and nowhere for my eyes to go, locked in an office with a movie star to whom I was not about to chronicle the details of my dismal existence. "So, Pachy, what's been going on with you?"

"Not much, I guess, I mean, nothing really," I said to the floor. She prodded, making small talk about the warm weather and playing outside. She asked about our football team while I looked closely at a picture on the wall of a stream running through a glen. Then she got to it.

"Tell me about Michael, Pachy."

I said, "He's in Wicks because he takes drugs." I was watching her out of the corner of my eye. She just looked at me and smiled.

"Pachy, do I make you nervous? You seem afraid of me. I have an 11-year-old son, and my husband says the two of us never shut up. So I have lots of experience talking to someone like you."

An 11-year-old? A husband? Ontiveras was supposed to be a movie star, with servants, with limos, with great hair. Not some mom with macaroni and cheese on the stove and bad breath in the morning.

The room suddenly became larger. I peeked a look. She was still very pretty, but the vapor trail left by her stardom had dissipated.

"Pachy? Are you all right?"

"What's his name?"

"Who?"

"Your son."

"Francisco, but we call him Frankie. I also have a daughter, Olivia. She is 8."

"That's how old I was when Mom died."

"I remember."

"I'm mad."

"About your mom dying?"

"Well, that too. But you asked me about Michael. I'm mad. The other kids talk about it at school. Buddy Bridges is always giving me, well, excuse me, he gives me crap."

"That's okay, Pachy. Say what you want."

My heart beat faster, and my eyes burned. I spoke in exhales, like a balloon with a tiny tear at the top. "My dad's always working, and Patrick, he's my older brother at college, he never calls, and when he does he's always telling everybody what to do. Aunt Merlene, Mom's sister, she fights with Dad. And Michael, he just goes in his room or to Prospect and takes drugs and doesn't say anything to anybody. It makes me so mad. Nobody cares but me."

I sat up in my chair and looked at my knees because they felt wet. I had been crying. I looked at Dr. Ontiveras. She was smiling at me. "Do you want a Kleenex, Pachy?" This was almost too much for me to bear: my secrets revealed, my movie star therapist exposed, and my manhood shamed.

I wiped my hands across my face and said, "I'm okay."

"You sure are, Pachy Kavanagh."

We spent the rest of the hour talking about her Frankie and Olivia and my mom. I tried not to give away too many secrets, but when I talked I felt like I was running downhill, gaining speed, the wind at my back. My mouth could hardly keep up with my mind.

At 4:30, Dr. Ontiveras said we should probably stop. I was a little embarrassed because it seemed I had been chattering the whole hour. I agreed and slowly made my way to the door, where I paused with the handle in my hand. "Pachy, would you like to come back tomorrow, instead of waiting until Monday? Besides, Thanksgiving is next week, and we'll miss a time."

I shrugged. "Sure." The handle was heavy in my hand. I stood for a moment.

"Pachy, sometimes I tell the kids I talk to that, if they want, I'll give them a hug. Would you like a hug?"

I shrugged again, then checked the hall for any spies, lest I be caught hugging a therapist, even a pretty one. I shuffled across the room.

It was a half hug, me turning to the side and leaning my head against her, nothing like my mom and I had perfected, but enough that I knew school Friday couldn't get over fast enough.

❦   ❦   ❦

I sauntered home, arguing with myself whether I should have spilled my guts to Ontiveras or just been "okay" for the entire hour. What would Moochie or Jackson have thought if they had seen me hugging her? Heck, maybe they hug their regular doctors.

I poked along, feeling strange but good. At the corner near Pinehurst Park, all that would change.

The sun was fading, and long shadows threw themselves across Sycamore Street. I could see my shadow, my backpack bulging like some alien attached to my neck, my body long and lean.

I took a left on Brookline, my street, and glanced across it to see a few people still playing in the park. Squinting into the bright sun, I headed up Brookline. After a couple of feet, I put my hand up to block the sun only to find the sidewalk filled with Buddy Bridges, flanked by Seth Carver and Robbie Snyder, the two wannabe hooligans who played backup for Buddy on the playground when Moochie Clark stood up to them.

Buddy spoke first, as usual. "Hey, Pack Rat. About time for you to be home, isn't it? Does your babysitter call the German Gestapo if you're late?"

I tried to walk around them, but a large ash tree filled the space between the sidewalk and the four lanes of Brookline, and a hedge pinned me in on the left. Buddy had planned very well. My mouth went dry. I could hear myself breathing.

Buddy stepped toward me. I shuffled back, but Robbie came around behind me, his hands resting on my backpack.

"Thought your stupid little Halloween stunt was pretty funny, huh, Kavanagh? Did dopey Mike teach you all those tricks? What about it, Pack Rat?"

"Just let me go home, Buddy. I didn't do anything to you."

"But you know who did, I bet," he snarled, looking at Seth and Robbie for confirmation of what he considered a complete thought.

"I don't know who did it. Just let me go home." I started forward, but Robbie held my backpack and Buddy and Seth grabbed my arms. I twisted, and they let go.

"Payback is tough, Pack Rat," Buddy said. He reached out with his right hand and suddenly slapped me hard on the side of my face. They laughed as I fought tears. "Hey, Robbie, what's in the bag?"

Robbie tore my backpack off, unzipped every tiny compartment and turned it over. Out fell math homework and a social studies book and pencils and lunch money and a folder of work and a junk pocket and a picture of my mother. I reached down to get the photo, taken when she was sick only a few months. She still had her hair and her radiant skin. Buddy stepped on it, grinding his foot into the sidewalk. He picked up the photo and looked at it with his usual simper. He threw it at me and said, "Pretty good-looking woman, once, I suppose." Buddy and Seth laughed. Robbie looked at them, then at me.

I clutched the photo, now scraped, my mother's beauty blistered by Buddy's foot and concrete, her blue eyes torn away, her smile dissected, her hair smudged and dirty. Only Buddy laughed.

From deep inside, I leaped, my hands clawing into Buddy's face. He screamed. I clawed deeper, now roaring from a well of anger and grief, or maybe it's all the same thing. He tried to pry me off but couldn't. In a violent moment, a huge, crashing force hit me from behind. I fell forward on top of Buddy, his flesh still in my fingers. The force then fell on me. Robbie, I figured, but as I glanced up, he and Seth were running down Brookline. Buddy was still screaming.

Somebody pulled me from the pile, and I stumbled, falling to my knees. Buddy, now crying loudly, crawled to his feet and staggered away.

Jackson Fowler's hand came to rest on my head, and I looked up in time to see him smiling.

"Thanks," I said.

CHAPTER 8

A Victory for Mr. Fowler

After Jackson helped me up, I checked to see if I still had all of me, which is a good thing when you misplace a few minutes. You never know what happens when you lose it because that's what you lose: knowing what's happening.

Buddy had pounded on my head and shoulders while I was digging my fingers into his face. The tip of my right index finger was purple. A pencil tip of blood oozed from underneath the nail; it hurt like a poke in the eye.

"You okay, man?" Jackson asked. God loves a good and dedicated athlete. Me, too. He had been shooting baskets after school with Joey Sindelar when some sixth graders said Buddy had gone looking for Robbie and Seth because they were going to "get" me on the way home from school. Jackson came looking for me, too.

What a stupid word—get. How about pound, beat, attack, avenge (provided anyone but Moochie and I knew), bully or even smack? Get? Please. I hurt more than a "get."

Surveying the cranial damage, I found no blood, but I had some sore spots and one sizable bump above my left ear.

I knelt down to pick up my junk, when an old woman poked her head over the hedge. "Young man?" she said insistently.

Jackson and I turned. He was a jump shot up Brookline retrieving some of my papers. "Yes, ma'am?" I stammered, sure that she had Traynor's finest en route to a fight. Maybe Michael and I could room together at Norwalk State Prison.

"Are you all right, young man? Do you need something?"

"No, I'm okay."

"I saw the whole thing from my kitchen window," she said with an unsteady swivel and gesture toward the back of the house about 20 feet beyond the hedge. "Those terrible, terrible boys. And your friend here to help you. My! Well, I never. I'm Mrs. Calhoun of the Litchfield Calhouns, and I saw the whole thing. Do you or your friend need anything?"

"No, thank you, ma'am." My mother taught me that being polite in the face of even the direst travesty always counts for something, especially with elderly women.

"Did you know those boys?" she said to me, then glanced at Jackson, who had joined us at the hedges.

"They go to my school."

"Dear, you give me their names, and I'll see to it that they will see the rubber hose tomorrow."

"Well…we know them but don't know their names. We've only seen them," I said, deciding both to lie and represent Jackson in the process. Dealing with Buddy requires a tight circle, Mrs. Calhoun's generosity and account notwithstanding.

Mrs. Calhoun looked perplexed, then past me to wave to someone. I turned and nearly lost my chef's surprise lunch. Ridgeway was making his way across the street with a woman his physical equal and a tiny dog the color of the pewter mug Grandpa Jack gave me for my First Communion.

"Sean, are you okay? Jackson? Mrs. Ridegway and I saw what happened from the park. Was that…"

"Hey, Mr. Ridgeway." I stopped him quickly, trying to save face in front of a Litchfield Calhoun.

"Arthur, these boys recognize the culprits from school. Is that your school, Arthur? But they don't know their names." I gave Mr. Ridgeway a sideways glance, then risked life and limb by staring directly into his massive, bearded face to tell him with my eyes what I couldn't with my mouth. He looked hard at me, frowned and then raised an eyebrow and finally shot a quick look at Jackson, an allegro attempt for information. Jackson's eyes scanned Mrs. Calhoun's hedge.

"Gladys," Ridgeway said calmly to Mrs. Calhoun, "Shereen and I can take care of this. We know Sean and Jackson. You can go inside."

"Well, all right, Arthur, if you think so. What are we coming to?" she said to no one in particular as she headed to the back porch, teetering a little on her cane. When she was out of earshot, Ridgeway spoke.

"Sean?" Ridgeway looked like he did when he caught you goofing off in music. I took a deep breath and explained that Mrs. Calhoun would never understand Buddy or my history with him. Ridgeway said he lived on the other side of the park and that this was his wife, Shereen, (two "nice to meet you, ma'ams" jumped from Jackson and me) and his dog, Placido. "I have no choice but to report what happened here to Mrs. Ploutz. You were assaulted, Sean. I should probably call the police."

"Oh, no, no, please, Mr. Ridgeway. I'm in enough trouble already." Well, my family was.

"For what? Minding your own business and defending yourself? I at least have to tell Mrs. Ploutz."

"That's gonna make it worse," I protested. "Buddy will find a way to get off with his dad."

"Not this time, Sean."

❦   ❦   ❦

Friday went from a day I couldn't wait for to one I was dreading. I took a hot shower and scrubbed off the attack as best I could. I avoided my father, and he left early as usual, so the few marks I had went unnoticed.

I walked to school with Jackson, who said he told his parents the whole story over pancakes at breakfast. Frank Fowler, a civil engineer and a no-nonsense guy, told Jackson he was going to come over and talk to Dad, but there wasn't time in the morning. He would do it tonight. I reminded Jackson that I was staying with them until my dad came home since he was going out of town today and he would be real late. Business, they thought; seeing Michael was the truth. He had spared me the trip, but said I would have to go to family week.

"You guys have a video player?" I asked, changing the subject.

"Yeah."

"Can I watch something on it tonight?" Jackson shrugged, as direct an answer for fifth grade as you sometimes get.

School was safe and routine because Buddy was gone, probably licking his face wounds. Ridgeway said nothing out of the ordinary to me either. I heard nothing from Ploutz.

I spent an hour with Ontiveras after school but said about a tenth as much as I did Thursday. She coaxed, but trust was something that did not come easy for me.

We decided I would come back Tuesday of next week since Thanksgiving was Thursday. I left quickly, before the subject of hugs came up.

I met Jackson, who had been shooting baskets, to walk home. Robbie and Seth were standing with a group of sixth graders outside school. They looked at me, then at each other and started toward us.

"Jackson…"

"I see them."

"Hey, Kavanagh, wait up." It was Robbie. We stopped. My heart raced. "Hey, man, Buddy said we were just going to scare you, talk to you, see if you know who made him sick on Halloween. I didn't know he would slap you or do that to your mom's picture. My mom was friends with your mom, from church. She's going to kill me tonight. Ploutz said she's going to call her." Ridgeway must have said something.

I shrugged. I think Robbie was apologizing. Seth just stood there. Robbie slouched for a moment, looking at the ground. He said, "If my mom calls your dad, tell her I didn't hit you, okay, Kavanagh, because I didn't." He left, shaking his head. Seth followed him back to the safety of the group. They all turned to look at Jackson and me. Jackson nodded in their direction. A couple of them nodded back, high-level communication in the geopolitics of fifth and sixth graders.

We ambled to Jackson's, where I was to eat dinner. Concealed in my backpack was *Going My Way*. I was hoping it would reveal some kernel of truth, some shifting symbolism that would explain my secret Santa's taste in gifts.

But Bing Crosby might have to wait. Buddy Bridges and his father were just getting out of their copper-colored Lincoln in front of Fowler's.

Jackson and I broke into a sprint, trying to head off the Bridgeses, but as we wheeled into his yard, we saw his father, who had been tending to a bush parched from the warm fall, shaking hands with Leon Bridges.

"Jackson. Pachy," came the acknowledgment of our arrival. Frank Fowler had never minced a word in his life. He was a paradigm of verbal economy. "You know Mr. Bridges and Buddy."

We nodded. They glared. Mr. Bridges was in a funeral black three-piece. Buddy was sporting khaki shorts, a blue short-sleeve button-down, and a face that looked like a sack of Thompson seedless red grapes.

"I'll get right to it, Fowler. I know John Kavanagh is out of town, checking on his son in drug rehabilitation, so I'll tell you. I'm considering legal action after what these two did to Buddy."

"What was that?" Frank said.

"What? Look at that face," Mr. Bridges shouted suddenly, sweeping his right arm back toward Buddy. I felt a giggle rattling around in my stomach. I made a face to keep it from moving any farther.

"From what I hear, and I mean no disrespect to Buddy, your son had it coming."

"Who told you that?"

"My son."

"Well, he piled on. No wonder."

"And Arthur Ridgeway. Called me not more than 30 minutes ago." My mouth fell open, but no giggle jumped out.

"He'll change his tune after I talk to him."

"You mean he lied to me?" Frank had taken a step closer to Mr. Bridges. It was a purposeful stride.

"He's mistaken. He told Ploutz…"

"No, he told me." Frank's gaze was locked.

"He was across the street in the park."

"But Mrs. Calhoun was right there. I called her."

"Who?" A small mustache of sweat was glistening on Mr. Bridges' upper lip.

"Mrs. Calhoun, of the Litchfield Calhouns." A faint smile etched its lines along Frank's mouth.

"Listen, Fowler, that Kavanagh kid is trouble. No mother, the father's always working. He has no discipline, no home life. A terrible temper."

"Pachy is no trouble. He tried to avoid it. Your son could learn a lesson from Pachy. Right now, I suggest you get out of my yard and go file whatever legal action you want. But before you do, you'd better ask Buddy to tell you the truth. That would be a good place to start your case. Good day, Mr. Bridges."

Leon Bridges stared hard at Frank Fowler, but Buddy was pulling on his sleeve. "C'mon, Dad. C'mon." His father harrumphed and complied.

Jackson and I looked at each other. Whoa!

We celebrated Frank Fowler's victory with fried chicken, mashed potatoes, and creamed corn.

"Jackson, did you leave the TV on?" Marian Fowler asked as faint voices from the darkened living room wafted into the kitchen.

"Oops, sorry Mrs. Fowler, that was me. I'll get it." I stood and headed to turn the TV off when the swift and sure grip of memory stopped me. I paused.

"Pachy?" Mrs. Fowler asked, a troubled tone to her question. I stepped to the doorway and then to the TV, where a scratchy, gray Bing Crosby was singing.

"Too-ra-loo-ra-loo-ral, Too-ra-loo-ra-li,

"Too-ra-loo-ra-loo-ral, hush now, don't you cry!"

I swallowed hard. "Pachy? Are you okay?" Mrs. Fowler asked again, now from the doorway.

"Too-ra-loo-ra-loo-ral, Too-ra-loo-ra-li,

"Too-ra-loo-ra-loo-ral, that's an Irish lullaby."

"Yeah, I'm fine. I thought I heard something." I reached up and turned the video player to off. I thought right. I had heard something, the Toola song Mom used to sing to us.

❦   ❦   ❦

Three days of school rushed by. Frank Fowler told Dad about Buddy and his dad. I saw Ontiveras. We had Thanksgiving at Aunt Merlene's. Michael was locked up in rehab, and Patrick was too busy studying for finals. Dad and I hung around for two hours, took some leftovers and endured Aunt Merlene's begging us to stay before we left.

Dad dropped me off. "You sure you don't want to come? I'm just checking a couple sites," he asked as I jumped out of the pickup.

"Nah. I'm gonna watch TV."

"I'll be home in an hour. See ya, Pack."

"See ya."

He drove off. I headed for the house, hoping another secret gift was cached near the door in the gathering dusk. I found nothing.

Except Michael, crouched and hiding behind a wicker chair in the corner of the porch.

CHAPTER 9

A Heartshake, Finally

If the hole in your heart doesn't heal right, the scar tissue can be as painful as the original wound. You're then destined to feel the same hurt over and over, in every circumstance, in every relationship, in every angle of life. Losing Mom put a hole in my heart, and even though Ontiveras told me I would heal and Dad said things were fine and I told myself I would be okay, I couldn't surrender another single thing.

But now, on the warmest Thanksgiving evening in 30 years, I was about to lose the skinny, frightened little boy who used to be my big brother. He looked small, a trembling little animal, hiding behind the white wicker chair.

"Michael! Geesh, Michael. Oh, no, man." I spit my words. My anger was obvious, my fear fueling it. I bounced on my knees like a wind-up toy. "What are you doing? You're gonna go to jail. Michael!"

"Pack, shhhsh. Listen to me. Pack! Listen, it's not what you think."

"Good, cuz I'm thinking bad, real bad." I shot a look across the street. The Fowlers had gone to Chicago to see Jackson's grandma. A darkening quiet hung over Brookline Street.

"I'm going back, tonight."

"Whyd'ja leave?"

Michael shrugged. I glared at him.

"Whyd'ja leave?" I insisted.

"I was thinking about running away, going to California with a guy. But I'm not."

"A guy? A guy? Who? Chip Smith? What about us? What about Dad? He thinks you're going to be better. Stay clean. Stay off Prospect. Geesh, Michael, I'm your little brother and I sound like Mom." I didn't mean to say it that way. It just came out. We both looked at the floor. A station wagon drove slowly past. I shuffled behind the pillar; Michael cowered back behind his chair.

Chip Smith was Michael's friend and I'm sure his drug connection, a clever hype and dealer who seemed to stay ahead of his parents and the police. Moochie told me Chip had tried to talk Michael out of Wicks.

"I'm going back. I want to stay clean. We had an in-town furlough, and I saw Rennie driving around and decided to go with him. I told them I'd be back in time, to cover for me."

"Where's Rennie?" Michael lifted his head in the direction of a stand of low evergreen bushes in need of a trim. Rennie Bismark sat on the ground between two bushes. He was smoking a cigarette, his yellowed teeth bared in a goofy smile. He waved, like a mayor in a Fourth of July parade, to no one in particular. I sneered and lifted my chin. He took a deep drag, his speed freak cheeks sucked tight against his mandible.

"You clean now? Michael?"

"Yeah. I had a beer, but Rennie wanted me to get high with him. I told him no. I don't want to go to jail, Pack. It scares me." He moved out from the chair to where I could see him. His head was covered in a black fuzz, his long hair therapeutically hewn by the staff at Wicks. He looked only slightly better than when he left.

"How long you been here?"

"'Bout 15 minutes. I got to get going. If I'm caught…well, I'll be in trouble." I could tell Michael was sparing me the truth of jail or prison.

"You'll go to jail."

"I gotta go." He braced himself with his hands and vaulted over the porch rail. He landed softly and motioned to Rennie. Then he turned to me and narrowed his gaze. "You can't tell anyone I was here, Pack, or I'm dead." He started to walk away.

"Michael." He stopped and turned. "I heard the Toola song, in an old movie. Mom used to sing it to us. Remember?" He looked at me, and for the first time in years I saw something in his eyes, a notation, a registration, a connection to the outside world.

"Whyd'ja come?" I said without demand.

He shrugged, shrouded now in dusk and smoke from Rennie's cigarette. "Wanted to see you." He smiled and walked away into the dark, and I knew, like I had never known anything before, that he would be caught and be sent to jail, or that he would change his mind and run, to be swallowed whole by California, sinking deep, deep into its teeming belly, or he would use and I would never see him again.

"Thanks," I said in a whisper. "Bye."

❦   ❦   ❦

December arrived and with it two days of chill winds and gray skies, but blue skies and 60s returned, prompting store owners to complain that the warmth had shoppers thinking of summer rather than running up a Christmas tab at their local retailers.

I had lain awake well past midnight on Thanksgiving, waiting for the phone to ring, the prison warden on the other end, telling Dad that Michael was settled in solitary. Or the Wicks guy saying Michael was a desperado, headed for California where he'll do desperate things, maybe even die. I awoke with a start at 3 a.m. from a dream. Mom was slicing turkey and singing the Toola song. I went to my door and listened. My bedroom window was open and a speeding vehicle racing down a black street whined just within earshot. I walked slowly down the hall and stood outside Dad's room. I could hear him breathing. I peered into the darkness. His clock radio illuminated the nightstand. No sign of calls. No notes. No phone books.

Michael must have made it. A surge of anger jumped inside me like a frightened calico. Now I was saddled with the dilemma of whether to tell and me being a below-average keeper of secrets. I knew this was one I would need to tell, but I knew it would cost my brother jail time.

Buddy stayed away from me at school, obviously heeding some power greater than him. We even sat next to each other without incident during an impromptu spelling bee. Not a word passed between us. The fifth-grade rumor mill, run with love and with great commitment by Sadie Scarvelli and Dawn Sczmak, reported that Buddy's father had had some sort of epiphany in the Fowlers' front yard, an enlightenment that cost Buddy friends and television for three weeks. Whatever works, I thought.

Dad was still gone a lot, so the rhythm of our lives didn't change much. Patrick called a couple times and talked about himself for 20 minutes, asked us how we were doing, and got off the phone before we could tell him. Dad hung up the extension, shook his head, and smiled at me as I put my receiver back in the cradle. I failed to see the humor.

No other secret gifts arrived, but Christmas was bearing down at school and at home. Ridgeway was busting chops and heads to make this year's program especially spectacular, so years hence, whenever Salton Elementary alumni gathered, they would praise the 1986 Christmas show.

I had family week to endure at Wicks. I hoped to get a few minutes alone with Michael to see how he made it back alive and then maybe punch him for making me keep such a horrible secret with so much on the line. Dad said Michael would come home December 23, the same day Patrick would arrive from college with his big ideas and small wardrobe.

I became a regular with Ontiveras, making Mondays, Wednesdays, and Fridays much more palatable for a kid who had a bad taste in his mouth from the first three and a half months of school. That changed on December 12, six days before Ridgeway's orchestrated triumph and the day before Dad and I drove to Wicks for family week.

"What is it, Pachy? You're hemhawing around, and we've been here 20 minutes. Do you want to talk about something else?" Ontiveras was into the dream thing again, and we were talking about Mom and carving turkey and singing.

"If I tell you something, like a secret, do you have to keep it? You can't tell anybody?"

"No, I can't, unless somebody is hurting you."

I weighed my options a moment more, adding to the moments since Thanksgiving when I figured I had to tell someone.

"Is someone hurting you, Pachy?"

"No."

"Then what…"

"I saw Michael," I interrupted with a breathy blurt, like a guilty witness confessing in court.

"I thought family week started Saturday."

"It does. I saw him on our porch, Thanksgiving night, after we went to Aunt Merlene's. Dad dropped me off and I saw him."

Ontiveras studied me. I looked at the floor. An oppressive silence filled the room, the silence you feel in confession after you admit your sins and the priest is devising your penance.

She waited me out. I told her everything down to the kind of cigarette Rennie was smoking (Marlboro, I think). I stopped and took a deep breath, knowing that Ontiveras and I were now inextricably linked by a shared secret.

Mom and I used to make pacts, promises she called heartshakes—like handshakes only with your heart. They were little things that only she and I knew like Audrey's real hair color and how Mrs. Finster had all that money. (Her husband buried it in the back yard, or so Mom said.) Mom had lots of them, secrets she would tell me, and then she would hold me close and say, "Let's warm up the shake so it will be forever." I looked at Ontiveras and realized I hadn't had a single warm heartshake since Mom died. Now I had a secret with Ontiveras.

"You won't tell, will you?"

"No, Pachy, I won't. But maybe you should tell your dad. He deserves to know."

I shrugged, finding it difficult to keep my eyes off the floor. "Pachy, is there something else? Are you afraid to tell your dad?"

"Yeah, kinda."

"Would you like me to help?"

"No. I can do it but maybe not right now."

"Sure, Pachy, but we'll talk about it before you do. Look, it's almost 4:30. We'd better stop so you can get home on time."

"Somebody keeps leaving me presents." I had plunged headfirst into uncharted seas, dived from a cliff in Acapulco into the swirling eddies of human connection. I had wagered my trust, and there was no turning back with Ontiveras. "A picture of my family and an old movie with a song Mom used to sing to get us to go to sleep."

"What?" she said with a puzzled smile.

I further unloaded my other great mystery, the red paper and the yellow bow, the camping picture, Bing Crosby, the identical cards, "To Pachy, Open before Christmas. With love."

I finished with, "Who do think is doing that?"

"I don't know, Pachy. Somebody who knows you and your family."

"Yeah," I shrugged. "I guess."

"And somebody who loves you, too." I looked at Ontiveras, my secret sharer. Maybe she left the presents.

"You better get moving. Good luck at family week. Remember what we talked about. I'll see you Monday. But if you really need to talk before then, call me at home."

✳   ✳   ✳

I trudged down the empty hallway, exhausted from forming new bonds with Ontiveras and spent from spilling secrets all over her floor. I heard a door open behind me as I neared the double doors at the end of the hall.

"Sean, wait."

"Oh, man," I thought, Ridgeway. I turned, knowing he was about to stick his gigantic face in mine and terrify me into a solo for the Christmas show or read me a list of grievances he had been hoarding. He arrived, beads of sweat on his forehead and a gasp expelling from his mouth somewhere behind his beard.

"Hey, Mr. Ridgeway."

"Sean, I wanted to tell you, away from class, how much I admire your courage and your perseverance. I know this has been a trying school year for you with your brother and this Buddy business. And I suppose you think I'm just one more teacher you have to endure. But I've been very proud of you. Have a good weekend…and get ready for Salton's best Christmas show ever."

He brushed past me and out the door. I stood staring after him, wondering what had just happened, wondering what my old life used to be like, before Mom died, before the world utterly changed in front of me.

CHAPTER 10

Passing Family Week, a New World Arrives

Mom said God was not in the business of making mistakes or junk. Those were the sole property of us humans. I asked her, if he was so good, why did he give her cancer? She said he didn't, only the strength to fight it, to live with it, and, in the end, to accept it.

When you're 11, most of that stuff flies over your head, a jet stream of adult talk heading to some distant place leaving only a dusting or a sprinkle for kids to understand. God plans it that way, I think. But 17 years later, as I remember my mother's look-death-in-the-face-every-day courage, I realize that perhaps I learned more the warmest December in Traynor history than in all the years since. As we become adults, maybe we don't actually get smarter about life and death and cancer and drugs and bullies and families. Maybe we just have more information.

Mom did say that God gave me to her—and Michael, Patrick and Dad, too (even Aunt Merlene)—and that God made families. In fact, she said, families were some of his best work, and when they fall apart it is the work of humans, and it makes God very sad.

"But, Mom, if you die, won't we fall apart?" I persisted on a windy summer day a month before she slipped away from us.

"No, Sweetie. You'll still be a family, and I'll still be with you, only in a different way." I had, as I usually did when Aunt Merlene or Dad didn't tell me not to, crawled into bed with Mom, snuggling as close as I could get, memorizing her touch and her warmth and her eyes and trying to ignore the awful smell of her sickness.

"I won't make you grilled cheese or tease Patrick about his shoes or flick Michael's hair out of his eyes, but I'll be here."

"When?"

"When Patrick curls his nose up like this when he is mad," she said making the tip of her nose wiggle back and forth. "Or when Michael insists on putting salt on his apples and watermelon. Or when you talk like you're 25 and ask more questions than anyone has answers for and hug somebody so hard that you become them and they you—that's when," she smiled. I laid my head on her tummy and smiled too, thinking maybe I understood.

"Don't let cancer take that away from us, Pachy."

"Okay," I said, her hand gently stroking the back of my head, inside of which I was furiously committing each molecule, each nanosecond, each nerve ending to memory.

❧   ❧   ❧

Family week at Wicks ended up being a merciful misnomer. We only had to be there part of Saturday and Sunday. Aunt Merlene insisted she tag along, and Dad capitulated, worn down by weeks of nagging. Her chatter made the hourlong trip seem longer, and to this day, I have no idea what she said.

The biggest surprise of family week was waiting for us on the steps of Wicks' Old Main, a square, two-story red brick affair with a courtyard filled with walkways, benches and low evergreen shrubs. Seven matching red brick cottages surrounded Old Main, so the place looked more like a college campus than a rehab center.

Patrick Kavanagh, striking a dashing pose as he leaned against a pudgy pillar, waved as we started up the steps.

"Dad, it's Patrick," I shouted, running up the steps to get to him first, knowing neither why I was so excited to see him nor what I would do when I got to him. I settled for an awkward lunge at his waist, supposedly a hug, but more of a tackle in reality.

"Whoa! Pack Man, easy."

"What are you doing here?" I blubbered, regaining my balance and what passed for composure.

"It's family week, right?" I knew Patrick would be able to make a head and tail out of this family week nonsense. He knew his way around smart people, and no shrink was going to get too cute with him.

Dad and Aunt Merlene joined us for a round of hugs. Dad said "thank you" to Patrick, one of those straight-in-the-eye jobs that made me believe Dad knew more than he was letting on.

Fifteen minutes later we all sat in a small room with Dr. Schiff, a nervous sort, with a body too big for his smock and a head too small for his rimless glasses.

"Michael will be here in a minute, so I thought I'd give you some ground rules," he said, looking at each one of us and then moving on to the next person. He'd done this before obviously. He said we would talk as a group about Michael's disease.

"Disease," I thought. "Man, not a disease, we've been through a disease."

The rest of the day Michael would talk to each of us individually. We could tell him what we thought about him and his drug use. His disease.

I didn't say anything unless I was asked. Schiff had to tell Aunt Merlene to put a sock in it a couple of times because she was dominating the conversation. Michael stared at the floor a lot, prompting Schiff to interrupt and force him to make eye contact. Twice Patrick took issue with Schiff's use of the word "therapy," and three times, after we got Aunt Merlene under control, there were long pauses when no one said a word, making Schiff even more nervous. Basically, it was a typical Kavanagh hatchet job. All we needed was Grandpa Jack to spill a drink and Audrey to blame it on Schiff.

We went to lunch in the cafeteria with the patients. They called them clients. I saw a few other miserable families sitting together, avoiding each other's eyes. I spent most of the afternoon watching TV and waiting for my turn to talk to Michael, who seemed lost with the entire exercise.

Schiff was still in the room when I walked in, but after some coaching, he left, giving me a chance to ask Michael about his near-escape.

"How'd you do it?" I said. He looked at me as if I had just grown a third eye. He leaned forward and said something very faint.

"Huh?"

"Pack, whisper," he rasped ever so slightly.

"How'd you do it?" I said, again, barely audible.

"Not now," he whispered, then sat back. I returned his knowing look, not knowing what he meant except for me to shut up about the escape. I would have to wait until Christmas.

We made small talk about the Toola song. I told him Jackson's mom and dad were watching a movie and I saw it. I was a little jumpy about lying in a place where some rooms have bars on the windows.

Schiff returned. He sat down in a whoosh, his white coat trailing him. He looked directly at me and asked how I felt about Michael's drug use. No intro. No small talk. No nothing. I answered with my customary shrug.

"You must have some feelings, Sean. Are you mad? Sad?" Schiff asked, subscribing to the theory that how I felt about Michael's plunge into powdery darkness was at my emotional fingertips, ready to delineate whenever anyone asked. Or that I had prepared some kind of family week statement. I knew coming here was a bad idea.

"I'm kinda mad, I guess," I offered without detail or passion.

"Sean, if you tell Michael how you feel, it will help him a lot," Schiff said. I shot a look at Michael, who was looking at me, his mouth twisted like he was readying to spit. "Michael and your family need you to tell him how you feel."

I looked at the floor, a scratchy institutional gray linoleum. I knew I wanted my family to be whole again, but I didn't know if I wanted to help Michael.

"I'm mad, that's all," I said, feeling like I'd lost my homework or got caught looking at Margaret Fletcher's test. Miraculously, the door opened. It was Patrick.

"I think he's been in here long enough. He's only 11. What do you want from him?" Patrick was staring hard at Schiff, who glanced at his clipboard.

"We're through here. See you in the morning, Sean," Schiff said. He didn't get to.

Patrick convinced Dad that I needed a big breakfast at the IHOP across the road from the motel and some Christmas shopping. Off we went, leaving the Family Group Session to Dad and Aunt Merlene.

According to the conversation in the car on the way home, no great shakes hurtled around the room, and Schiff pronounced Michael most likely fit to come home on the 23rd.

Patrick bought me a new sweater, and even though it was nearly 70 degrees, I wore it home. He never once asked me about how things were at home or if I missed Mom or how Dad was doing. He talked about college and his girlfriend Isabel from Portugal. I stared out the window watching the afternoon slip by at 65 miles per hour and wondered which I liked least: Schiff's prying or Patrick's indifference.

       ❦   ❦   ❦

I reported the details of family week to Ontiveras on Monday but could only stay a few minutes because Ridgeway had scheduled three days of after school dress rehearsals, and I was one of a group of fifth and sixth graders selected to help with crowd control for the younger grades. Our dress rehearsal was Wednesday but on Monday and Tuesday I would be riding herd on kinder-gartners, first, second and third graders.

"That sounds great, Pachy," Ontiveras said.

"Even if I only said I was mad?"

"Sure. That was your honest feeling, right?"

"Yup. You don't think Patrick's getting after Dr. Schiff will mean Michael's going to get in trouble, do you?"

"No, I don't, Pachy. So this is it until after Christmas vacation, right?" School was out for Christmas vacation Friday, and Ontiveras couldn't be there, so I wouldn't see her for three weeks.

"Yeah, I guess. Are you coming to the Christmas show?"

"Yes, I'm bringing my husband and Frankie and Olivia, too."

"Great," I said, apparently with enough resignation that Ontiveras noticed.

"You can call me anytime you need to talk, Pachy."

"Thanks," I said and started toward the door. I stopped, took a deep breath and turned. "Merry Christmas, Dr. Ontiveras."

"Pachy," she said, her arms out. I nearly sprinted for a hug, the first since I'd lost my mind in her office the day Buddy jumped me. Now she felt strong and warm. I squeezed a tear from falling. "Merry Christmas to you, too," she said.

Ridgeway's spectacular was everything it had been the year before and the year before that. Christine DeLaurier, a chatty third grader, threw up back stage causing a temporary gagging epidemic before the janitor could find a bucket of sawdust and some air freshener. Brody Duff, the tallest sixth grader at Salton, fell off the riser during *We Three Kings*, but recovered before the three wise men futzing with incense and myrrh in front of the chorus wet their pants laughing. The timing was divine intervention, but then, every elementary school Christmas show needs some guidance from thy perfect light.

Dad and Aunt Merlene and Uncle Ray, her shy husband, came to watch. Dad stayed through the entire show and even took my picture when Ridgeway allowed the parental paparazzi to come forward and flash away.

Afterward Ridgeway basked in glowing praise from well wishers. As I ran a broken field of parents and grandparents in the crowded gym, I stopped short. My dad was shaking Ridgeway's hand and talking to him. Without warning, Arthur Ridgeway, all 300 pounds of him, grabbed John Kavanagh, my borderline stoic Irish father, and hugged him.

As I stared from 10 feet away, Ridgeway caught my eye like a security guard catches a thief. He waved me over next to Dad and whispered in my ear. "Thanks, Pachy, for everything." Who knew?

The ride home was its usual quiet. One more day of school and four more days before Michael comes home.

"What did Ridgeway say to you?" I finally asked my father.

"Oh, nothing. He said you did a good job in the show."

"He called me Pachy. He's never done that," I said to my window. Dad was silent.

We pulled into the driveway and past the lighted porch, where a small red package with a yellow bow sat near the front door. It would unlock a new world for me.

CHAPTER 11

Letting Go Inside the Treasure Box

It's hard to know what's important—what to leave out, what to let in. Who gets space in your heart. Who gets to keep it. Sometimes you have to do the best you can with the information you have. It's hard to know.

But Mom knew. Absolutely.

I sat in the hall outside her room and listened one windy Wednesday morning when the end was close. Father Salem was in there, endlessly explaining to the world's most faithful person the importance of faith. Talk about redundancy.

When he finally paused, I heard Mom's voice. It was weak at first, but it gained clarity and strength.

"This whole thing, I think, this cancer and my life as a person of faith have taught me that the journey is one of figuring out what's important," she said.

"And how is that Mrs. Kavanagh?" Salem asked.

"It's a Corinthian knockoff, Father Salem." I imagined her smile. "That faith, hope and love business. Learning what's important is head, gut and heart...and the greatest of these is heart."

"Oh?" Salem said, sounding like he was challenging a dying woman.

"If it touches my head, requires my intellect, if it runs through my tummy where feelings sometimes reside, and if it needs my heart, which is infinitely expandable, if all three are there, then it must be important." She paused to gather breath. "The mind and intuition speak volumes, but sometimes the heart is simply enough to know."

"The brain can follow, too," Salem offered. "Matthew said, 'Out of the overflow of the heart, the mouth speaks.'"

"He did, didn't he," Mom said.

"Pachy!" A gale force whisper roared passed me. I was by then peeking around the corner into Mom's room and now jumped back. Aunt Merlene, hands on her hips, apron askew and eyes locked on me, was hovering above. "What are you doing? Are you snooping? That's private."

I shrugged. She continued to stare. Father Salem was backing out the doorway saying good-bye to Mom. He turned and looked at Aunt Merlene and then down at me and nodded. He headed for the stairs, Aunt Merlene scurrying behind. I leaned around the corner again.

She caught me, as I wished. "Hi, Sweetie. Come see me," Mom said. I jumped to my feet, ran across the room, and crawled into bed with her. She could hardly keep her eyes open.

"Are you sure, Mom?"

"Absopositivalutely," she said, making me murmur and giggle and hold her close.

"I was listening, to you and Father Salem."

"Mmm," she said, her eyes closed, her mouth turned up in a sweet smile. "What do you think?"

"What's important?"

"You, Pachy, that's what's important. And your brothers and father and Aunt Merlene and Grandpa Jack. The whole famdamily," she said, her smile widening.

"You're silly. How do you know?"

"You want me to show off a little?" she said. I sat up to look at her, her eyes now open, her smile the smile of a healthy person.

"Yeah. Show off."

"Here goes, Pachy Kavanagh, just for you, so always remember: 'Le Coeur a ses raisons que la raison ne connait point.'" Mom loved to speak French. She took three years in high school and went to France one summer with Susan Atwater. She used to raise her glass at dinner and announce, "Á votre santé," which would roll Dad's eyes.

"What's 'lay core raisins whatever' mean, Mom?"

"It means 'The heart has reasons that reason knows nothing of,' Pachy. Always remember."

Dad found the package when he checked the mail. He yelled up the stairs. "Hey, Pack. There's a Christmas present here for you."

I panicked. I had flopped on my bed for some veg time after the big Christmas show, but Dad's announcement catapulted me into the hallway and down the stairs. I grabbed the tiny present from the table in front of him, now with the newspaper and a beer.

"Whoa! What's the hurry, Pack? I read that card. 'To Pachy. Open before Christmas. With love.' You got a girlfriend, Pachy?" he said, a slight smile edging up on the left side of his mouth. I can't remember Dad smiling or laughing since Mom got sick. I'm sure he must have, but I don't remember. I stared.

He said, "Well?"

"Oh, no. Come on. This is just a secret Santa gift from somebody at school. We do that every year. Just a little thing."

"With love?"

I shrugged. He laughed, a short, compact snort, but it was a laugh. I sat down, holding the gift but now more interested in my father's good humor.

"What's so funny?" I said, hoping to milk it, to stretch into a minute or an hour or an evening, this new father, the one with the smile.

"You, Pachy. You are such a little grown up until it comes to grown up things. Then you're my baby boy, 11 and every day of it."

"Well, I don't have a girlfriend," I said, now talking to my dad just for the sake of talking. That's what we did for an hour, until he got up said it was bedtime. We talked about the show and sports and Patrick and Aunt Merlene and Mrs. Pilcher and Christmas and his pickup. Mom and Michael didn't make the list, but it was the best hour I had spent with him in more than three years.

I closed my bedroom door and ripped into the tiny gift, smaller than the card and weightless. Inside was a box the size of a glue stick and taped shut. I popped it open, folded back the cotton, and found a shiny gold key. I held it up, examining every detail. It was about 2 inches long, with a notch on the business end and a worn oval at the top. It was shiny but well-used, like a freshly scrubbed kitchen floor.

I tried it in my door and the trunk in the corner, but neither responded. I tried locks all over the house, but the day and night had sapped me, so I put the key back in the box, dropped it into the bag I kept hidden under my bed, and crawled under the covers.

Before morning, I had opened a steely vault whose insides dripped with jewels and sparkling doubloons, unlocked a gigantic tome called the "The Book of Knowledge," and opened the door to an endless showroom of cool cars and fancy toys.

Michael arrived home with little fanfare on December 23. Dad went to pick him up. I stayed home and waited for Patrick who burst through the door 15 minutes before Michael made a sheepish entrance. We all slapped around and exchanged Kavanagh men greetings, something between a lean and a push but definitely not a hug.

Dad took us to the Brick Bar, where we ate steaks and home fries and made plans for Christmas Eve and Christmas Day.

Michael didn't say much, but he did follow the conversation, a vast improvement. He caught me staring at him a couple times at dinner, but he just smiled. We decided Michael and Patrick would buy a tree and do some shopping on Christmas Eve. We'd all decorate it and then go to midnight Mass. We used to do this every year, with Mom at the helm and us her dutiful first mates. It had been four Christmases.

I got up late Wednesday, Christmas Eve. Mrs. Pilcher had made everybody breakfast and saved me some. Patrick and Michael were reading the paper. Dad was at work, trying to finish a job before the weather changed, a warning we watched on television the night before.

"Hey, Pack," Patrick said, putting down the business section. "Thought you might sleep through Christmas. Pilcher here has outdone herself. Better dig in. I'm hitting the shower and then Michael and I are going to buy the best tree in Traynor." He disappeared up the back stairs.

"Hey," I said to Michael, who smiled back. Pilcher was pushing a wash rag across the counter when a car horn blared from the driveway.

"Ooo. Der iz my ride, boys. Merry Chrizmaz," she yelled and waved as she bounded out the back door. The kitchen went stone silent. I began to eat.

I could feel Michael looking at me. "Two guys covered for me," he started. I looked up and saw his eyes first. "I snuck back in through the kitchen and made it to my room without anyone seeing me. I had to pay Ralph the cook $20. Rennie drove me to the service entrance. I hid under a blanket in the back of his car. He pretended to have kitchen stuff from an earlier delivery. He talked his way in. I was lucky. I could have gone to jail. It still scares me."

I looked at Michael. Now fully informed, I was no less angry that he would risk everything for a beer and a ride with Rennie.

"Glad you made it," I said, managing some brotherly compassion.

"You haven't told anyone, have you?"

"Nope," I lied.

"It's good to be clean, Pack. It's good to be home. I hope someday you'll forgive me for everything. They told me I can't expect it all at once, but I hope someday you can."

The room went silent again. He waited, looking at me, something I wasn't used to. "Me, too, Michael," I said.

Then the world changed again. He stood up and walked over to me, two slices of bacon and half a piece of toast in my mouth. He leaned over and kissed me on the top of my head. "Thanks, Pack. I'm going to shower." I was without speech—me, Sean Kavanagh, who was mouthier than anyone I knew.

After they left, I fiddled around waiting for Dad. I finally went to his room, jumped on the bed and grabbed the TV remote. I stared at daytime TV, flipping through holiday specials and two channels with *Miracle on 34th Street*. I rolled over and closed my eyes.

When I opened them, I saw it clearly. I ran to my room, fished the gift key from the bag under my bed, and ran back. It fit perfectly, unlocking Mom's treasure box with a sweet snap.

Dad found me in the corner of his room, a low moan bubbling from inside, my shirt soaked. I was inconsolable. I had tried to stop, but sadness crashed in on me, wave after wave. The bedspread was wet with tears. I was so hysterical, he called Dr. Ontiveras.

She found us sitting on the bed. In a neat pile was jewelry, pictures, perfume, two marbles, a silk scarf and a card that said, "To

Pachy, Merry Christmas, With Love, Mom." I rubbed my hands on the card over and over again.

"What's this mean?" I said between sobs to Ontiveras, in jeans and a sweatshirt.

"It means your mother loved you, Pachy."

"What about the gifts?"

"What gifts?" Dad wondered aloud. I went to my room and returned with the gifts and the cards. He examined them as if they were works of art. It felt good to share them. So good that I told Dad about Michael hiding on the porch. He promised not to be mad.

He wasn't either and hasn't been since. Ontiveras left before Michael and Patrick came back with a tree and some packages. I stayed upstairs, Dad convincing my brothers that I was sick to my stomach. I cried all afternoon, Dad there most of the time to hold my head.

He brought me dinner and asked about church. I nodded.

❦   ❦   ❦

An angel watched over me that Christmas Eve 1986, some guardian. I made it through midnight Mass, where, at the Sign of Peace, when we Catholics greet each other, my normally impassive father, John Kavanagh of Kavanagh and Sons Contractors, took me in his strong and able hands and hugged me close and hard and real. "I love you, Pachy," he whispered.

Wendall Stallmeyer, three shots of whiskey into the holiday, waved to us after Mass. "Warm, for Christmas, ain't it, John?"

I smiled. It finally was for me.

CHAPTER 12

What We Did with the Rest of Our Lives

I wish I had a happy ending; I have neither. Seventeen years later, Dad seems happy. Patrick still knows it all, only more of it. Aunt Merlene has slowed down a little, but was at my house the other day suggesting I rearrange the furniture.

I don't know about Michael.

Nor are the Kavanaghs without end. My wife, Jennifer, and I welcomed our first-born to the clan 18 months ago. He's the first thing on my mind when I awake and the last thing on it before I fall asleep. I never thought I had the chops to be a father, but like Mom said, the heart is infinitely expandable. I have found plenty of room for our son.

I'm luckier than most people, having my first difficult lesson at 11 about life and death, heart and reason, and holding on and letting go. Sometimes it takes years. That's not a recommendation—unless you are emotionally masochistic. But Christmas

1986 changed me forever and gave me a safe place to put my mother and my family.

This would also be a much better Christmas story if, when we walked out of midnight Mass, a gentle snow had been falling. But Traynor stayed warm for six more days. A blizzard descended on New Year's Eve, dumping 10 inches of snow and stranding Patrick, who ranted for 24 hours before escaping on Jan. 2.

Dad was home more than he was at work during my Christmas vacation, leaving Uncle Mick to run the business. Michael told me it was because Dad didn't trust him. "Gee, ya think?" I said, risking a smack to the melon or a fist to the arm because, for a few weeks there, Michael acted more like a brother than I ever remember.

I didn't trust him either; he was trying, though. He went to a meeting a day and two of them sometimes for the three weeks he stayed with us. He even called somebody about working on his GED. But when you teach people how to treat you for years, the learning curve can be steep. Michael shouldn't have expected us to trust him.

What happened to me Christmas Eve, after the key opened Mom's treasure box, remains jumbled, part psychoanalysis, part mystery. An explanation is not original; Ontiveras did all the heavy lifting on that. She said, after Mom died, I confused the words of well-meaning old ladies from the Altar Society and gruff subcontractors who knew Grandpa Jack with good, healthy grieving. When they said I needed to "be strong," about the best an 8-year-old could come up with is don't cry or act like a sissy.

She said I used three things to survive—isolation, football and making sure my family appeared to be functioning beyond small town embarrassment standards—but none of them worked. Three years was about as long a gig as I could put together. That's why I leaked tears at practice after I went nuts tackling Joey Sindelar. It's why the first time I trusted Ontiveras, I wept without hardly noticing. It's also why when I looked inside the treasure box and found a card to me from Mom, it ruptured the dam, the "be strong" barrier.

At least that's what Ontiveras said—then and later—and sometimes you have to trust people. I still call her once in a while for a chat. After Christmas 1986, I remained a regular until junior high. Then I saw her about once a month and then…well…sometimes I call.

That was the reason part. The heart part was more mysterious, but I'm more comfortable with it. I think Ontiveras is, too, but her training and experience work against her.

The treasure box was my ticket out of holding on, feeling ashamed, thinking everyone else was thinking my family and I were weird. The first stop was an enormous sadness, and what kid wants that? But death is sad, so your heart needs to talk to your mind. When mine did one warm Christmas Eve, I wept for nearly 10 hours, a good start to getting on with the rest of my life.

For years, I tried to solve the mystery of the three gifts, unwilling to accept Dad and Ontiveras' solution, that Mom had left them. Reason told me otherwise. They were just appeasing a distraught fifth grader. But I knew dead people didn't wrap gifts or write cards or buy videos.

Slowly though, my heart came to accept the gifts as the end of my holding on, the beginning of my letting go, and the way of keeping my mother's memory—and now Michael's, too. I thought a perfect family, without drugs and discord and dysfunction, would keep her close. Anything else and we would lose her. Hey, I was a kid.

Years later, I decided that it didn't matter who or how the gifts arrived on my front porch, only that they did. I can live with that mystery—that Christmas wonder.

❦   ❦   ❦

We lost Michael. He never made it. We have no idea where he is or even if he's alive. No one has seen him or heard from him in seven years, but it's a death, one that only a miracle could undo, a miracle we hope and pray for but have long since quit planning our lives around. We lost him long ago, I guess. His clean six months starting Christmas 1986 tantalized us, lured us into thinking he had beaten his disease. It made his last descent into hell that much more difficult.

About three weeks after Christmas, he landed a spot in a halfway house in Astoria and a job stocking shelves at an Albertson's. The police required both. We saw him about once a month. He came home for Easter, his hair long again, his gaze less steady than at Christmas, but still, he seemed happy.

On May 17th, his counselor at the halfway house called, said Michael had run away and that he had no choice but to call the police. Joe Detering stopped by the next week and asked to talk to Dad in private.

"Whatever you have to say about Michael, you can say in front of Pachy, Joe. He's been through the wars with this thing," Dad said. Joe nodded.

"Technically, Michael's a fugitive," Joe said. "But we're not really interested in pursuing him or having somebody else pursue him. If he comes back to Traynor, then we would have to talk. I know he's sick, John, and what he was holding was nothing really, but we can't tell what a judge might do. There are hard cases in the department who'd think he should be locked up. You know that."

"But he went to Wicks like you wanted," I said.

"I know, Pachy, but he needed to complete some other steps. Sorry, buddy."

Michael had run off to California, his original plan to beat his demons. The problem was wherever you go, there you are. At least that's what he said when he called from the sunshine and needed money. Dad sent him some and some more and some more. Ontiveras helped Dad switch meetings from cancer survivors to parents whose kids are living in the pit of addiction. He still sent money.

Then one time he didn't. Then another time. Nor did I, having been to a few of those meetings with Dad. Michael quit calling. That was 1995.

A year later, on a breezy summer night, I pulled into my driveway, where a tattered homeless man stood staring at his feet. His left hand was shoved deep into his pocket, his right behind his back. Matted, greasy hair bounced the porch light from his head. His beard was stubble, like a barren field where life had stopped before it ever bloomed.

I stepped out of my car, a little curious, a little unsure.

"Pack Man," he rasped, a cigarette he had held behind his back now moving to his lips.

My body stopped working for a moment. I tried to blink an odd dizziness away. I struggled for the breath to talk. "Oh man, oh my God, Michael."

"Yeah. Michael, little brother." I moved closer. He was rail thin and ancient, his eyes sunken. A car parked down the block honked. He stuck one, bony "just a minute" finger in the air. "I need to get back to California, Pack Man. Can you help me out?"

Telling Michael "no" on the phone was easier than in my driveway, where he stood dying before me.

"Come inside, Michael. I'll get you some help."

"No. I'm past all that now." He sucked deep on the smoke. "So can ya help me?" He avoided my eyes. I fished $13 out of my pocket. That wouldn't take him far whether on the road to California or to another of a million rushes for which he was paying with his life.

"Thanks, Pack," he said, moving past me in a wide half circle. At the end of the driveway, he turned, flicked his cigarette and said loudly. "You know, Pachy, sometimes I still sing the Toola song. I remember it, when Mom sang it to us. And I sing it…See ya, Pack Man."

He walked slowly into the darkness. No one has heard from him since. That was seven years ago.

❧   ❧   ❧

Ridgeway left Salton after the 1986 Christmas show. A new music teacher greeted us when we arrived back from vacation. Ridgeway took Shereen and Placido and retired in Arizona. As I sat on the bed with Dad and Ontiveras on Christmas Eve, I came to know Ridegway's double life and how it saved the Kavanaghs.

"I have some secrets, too, Pachy," Dad said after I had shown him the gifts and told him about Michael. "Dr. Ontiveras here introduced me to some guys who lost their wives to cancer, too. I've been talking to them. Sometimes at night when I get home late, I've been talking to them. Saturday mornings, too. And I feel better."

I looked at my father and tried to remember if he had ever shared a secret with me.

"And guess what?" he continued. "Mr. Ridgeway is the group leader. His first wife died 22 years ago, but he still goes because it helps him."

"Dad and Ridgeway? Oh, no. Surely, I'm dreaming," I thought. It did explain the hug after the Christmas show and the odd conversation I had with Ridgeway when we were alone in the hallway just before Christmas vacation. I looked at Ontiveras, who nodded her assent to Dad's newfound therapy.

Grandpa Jack died on the 14th green at Cypress Gardens Golf Course in Florida two weeks before I graduated from high school. Audrey caused a minor scandal in Traynor and nearly sent Aunt Merlene past the breaking point when she wore a pastel peach number to the funeral. "Bad taste, stupidity and disrespect, all rolled into one," Aunt Merlene hissed at Dad from the pew behind us during the service. Audrey also got a little tipsy at the wake, but then, hardly anyone notices such things at an Irish wake. Of course, Aunt Merlene did.

Jackson Fowler played college football on scholarship and became an electrical engineer. Buddy Bridges is the youngest member of Bridges, Ellis, Haverford and Bridges. This after his father nearly had to build a wing onto Farmington Law School to get Buddy accepted. I see him occasionally, and I'm cordial. It's always an unreciprocated act. I never fail to notice, too, the tiny scar just below the arc of his left eyebrow.

Patrick married Isabel in a ceremony somewhere in Europe. We had a party for them when they came back, but they spent most of the evening arguing with Mr. Fowler about trade tariffs and gun control. They are childless on purpose, and both teach at a small college in Vermont, content that SUVs are ruining the world, that free range something is better than regular, and that performance art can save us. They come to Traynor once a year for a perfunctory three days.

Dad made me his priority after the treasure box incident. I used to think it was because he was scared that something awful would happen, but I've come to believe that it was because it was the right thing to do. And that he loved me. He still worked hard, but he never missed another game or school event and made a pest of himself when I was in high school. I loved it but put up a good front for my friends.

Dad still goes to the office but only to have an excuse to go to morning coffee with his cronies and spend the rest of the day with his grandson. Uncle Mick's kids, my cousins Ryan and Tim, run the business. Having never driven a nail straight in my life, Kavanagh and Sons was no place for me.

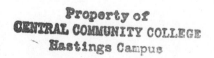

❉   ❉   ❉

I went to college to be a businessman and left as a teacher, which I am, in fifth grade where all the action is, where most kids still like school, and where my life changed forever.

Every day, I miss my mom—her touch, her smile, her absolute unconditional love, her goofy faces, her knowledge of heart and reason. I miss her unabashed faith. I miss her oneness with the rest of the world: how she knew which way the currents of life were flowing and how she set us in our little Kavanagh dinghy so we could enjoy the ride.

But every day I see her, too, most in Michael Clare Kavanagh's blue eyes when I wake him in the morning. I see her in his wont to throw food around the kitchen and capture your heart at the same time. I see her in his unconditional love. I see her in the treasure box on his dresser filled with a toddler's trinkets and a note from his father in French.

I sing him the Toola song when I put him to bed at night, him gurgling in his crib or nestling in my arms. And I never finish the lullaby without thinking about Michael.

0-595-32776-1

Printed in the United States
21729LVS00005B/160-231